The Bill

The Bill 6

JOHN BURKE

Thames Mandarin

A Thames Mandarin Paperback

THE BILL 6

First published in Great Britain 1992
Reprinted 1992
by Mandarin Paperbacks
Michelin House, 81 Fulham Road, London SW3 6RB
in association with
Thames Television International Limited
149 Tottenham Court Road, London W1P 9LL

Mandarin is an imprint of the Octopus Publishing Group,
a division of Reed International Books Limited

A CIP catalogue record for this title
is available from the British Library

ISBN 0 7493 1178 9

Phototypeset by Intype Ltd, London.
Printed and bound in Great Britain
by Cox & Wyman Ltd, Reading, Berks

One

It was a day of some rejoicing for a couple of the Sun Hill team. Police Constable Dave Quinnan had every reason to feel pleased with himself. Chief Superintendent Brownlow was in equally good mood: there had been rather a lot of fall-out from complaints higher up in recent times, and it made a nice change to have one of his men officially commended instead of being reprimanded. Brownlow spent several minutes tweaking at the cuffs and buttons of his uniform and checking that his hat was on at the right angle before setting off to Area Headquarters. He hoped he could rely on Quinnan himself making an effort to be smart and for once keeping his naturally facetious nature throttled down. 'A proper demeanour,' was the Chief Super's much quoted definition of one essential virtue in a serving officer.

Sergeant Tom Penny was not among the happy ones. It was Penny who had arrested the child murderer and hauled him in. Tom Penny was the one the sad, twisted little killer had trusted, insisting on his doing the slow, sickening questioning that led at last to conviction. Yet the award was going to Quinnan. Because Quinnan had put on his sharp, know-all act, cutting corners and then coming up smelling of roses. And because nobody, in either the lower ranks or the higher ranks, much cared for Penny. That was about the size of it. Today they were carefully not looking at him; not wanting to risk his comments; not daring to mention Quinnan and the sort of guff that was being poured all over Quinnan this afternoon.

Penny made sure of taking his lunch break in the farthest

corner of the canteen, sitting at an angle so that nobody would venture to grab a chair beside him or on the other side of the table.

While PC Quinnan, no doubt, was knocking back the smoked salmon and the white wine and being patted on the back. He could only hope the smart-arse would dribble the wine all down himself, or preferably spew the lot down the DAC's best trousers.

Dave Quinnan was in fact just what Brownlow had hoped for. He arrived trim, scrubbed, and appearing very taut and well disciplined. As he helped his mother and girlfriend out of the taxi outside Area Headquarters, he managed to look as if he made a habit of travelling in taxis rather than racketing about the manor in a panda car, and tipped the driver with offhanded generosity. Gallantly offering an arm to each of his companions, he led them in great style up the steps to the glass doors.

They were escorted by a suitably deferential WPC to a large room where a long buffet table had been set up against one wall. Chief Superintendent Brownlow was already there, with a glass in his hand. In one field of activity, anyway, he could be relied on to get his priorities correct. Patronizingly he moved towards the newcomers.

'Found it all right, then, Quinnan.'

Damned stupid remark, really. But Quinnan was on his best behaviour, not venturing even the slightest cocky facetiousness. 'Yes, sir.' He drew the two ladies forward, really cutting a dash. 'This is Suzanne – my young lady.'

Brownlow gravely shook hands.

Suzanne was blonde and tall and leggy, and had chosen to wear the skimpiest possible current fashion to display those legs. Her lipstick momentarily glued her lips together, but her eyes simpered and after a moment she was able to say: 'Pleased to meet you, I'm sure.'

'And my Mum,' said Quinnan.

6

Brownlow sketched a hint of a polite bow this time as he shook hands.

'And you're Inspector Monroe, aren't you?' said Mrs Quinnan. 'David's told me so much about you.'

Quinnan gulped. Brownlow forced a smile. 'Chief Superintendent Brownlow, actually.' He kept the smile in place. 'You must both be very proud.'

'Oh, yes.' Mrs Quinnan's plump, eager little face was aglow. She contrived to be nervous but radiant at the same time. 'Well, catching a murderer, that's about the best you can do in this job, isn't it? I mean, I said to our David, they can't ask more of you than that.'

'No, quite.' Brownlow allowed himself a twinkling glance at the embarrassed PC.

Other officers arrived, some accompanied by wives, mothers and girlfriends, all making rather feverish conversation and trying to balance glasses and small plates while sorting out who was who and who to be most respectful to. A female press officer with a tight blouse and a large bottom edged with an official photographer between one group and another, appraising them and perhaps wondering how to make the best of a none too inspiring job.

Brownlow drifted away to make his mark with Divisional Assistant Commissioner Jago. It had always been an uneasy relationship: good fellowship on the surface, with some treacherous undercurrents capable of dragging you down when you least expected it.

Mrs Quinnan pointed Suzanne towards a piece of creamy pink gateau on the table, but Suzanne shook her head. It had been difficult enough squeezing into that shred of a dress. She was determined to be a weight watcher for some considerable time yet.

'It was automatic, really.' Another PC, looking as unnaturally tidy and restrained as Quinnan, was modestly disclaiming any right to be lining up here for an award. 'I just ripped off my shirt and bound his arm up in it. And then just sat

7

there with him till the ambulance turned up. They managed to sew it back on, so I suppose it was worth it.' He generously offered Quinnan a chance to declare his own unworthiness. 'How about you?'

Dave Quinnan shrugged.

Mrs Quinnan was not going to leave it at that. 'He caught Donald Blake,' she proclaimed. 'You know, the Sun Hill child-killer.'

The young man was surprised and impressed. 'That so?'

'I saw a bit of evidence and put two and two together, that's all.'

The DAC and his superintendent were bearing down upon them with Brownlow in pursuit, determined not to allow himself to be left out of earshot.

'Mervyn the Mongrel, eh?' said DAC Jago. 'The big red dog?'

Quinnan shook hands. 'That was it, sir.'

'Excellent work.'

Mrs Quinnan beamed. Her son said: 'We do our best, sir.'

Inevitably there had to be a speech before the presentation of the awards. Inevitably the speaker would be the DAC. As silence was called for and Jago cleared his throat, something like Quinnan's old lopsided sneer crept into the corner of his mouth. But he caught his mother's eye, and it had more of an effect on him than anything that Brownlow, Conway or Monroe could have thrown at him. Putting his glass down, he tried to look serious and attentive.

'Ladies and gentlemen.' The DAC was usually curt and snappish in conversation. Today he had decided that the occasion merited a slow, grave tempo. 'Occasions like this are the lifeline to sanity which makes the thankless lot of a DAC worth while.' Thankless, thought Quinnan disloyally without the flicker of a facial muscle, but not moneyless. 'Nowadays I seem to spend a lot of my time defending the good name of the Metropolitan Police. *You* are my reassurance. The proof, if proof were needed, of the courage, alertness and dedication of the men and women who *are* the Metropolitan Police. You are the reason why the people of London can have faith and confidence in the service we provide. For although you have been, quite rightly, singled out for individual honour, you are in one sense merely the representatives of the thousands of your colleagues who day in, day out, perform their duties with similar courage, alertness and dedication. For no other reason than that it is their job. *The* job.'

It went on predictably for a further five minutes. Mrs Quinnan drank it all in with open mouth and shining eyes, sharing her attention between the speaker and her son. Suzanne shifted her weight from one leg to the other, not unaware that one of the constables with a particularly podgy wife was eyeing her covetously.

When the time came for the commendation certificates to be handed out, the routine was the same for each recipient. Two women and seven men stepped forward in turn, took the certificate with the left hand, and paused in mid-handshake with the DAC while the photographer took a picture.

Suzanne, half hypnotized by the unfaltering stare of the man who, it transpired, had saved two old ladies from the attacks of a mad rottweiler launched at them by a neighbour of equal madness, became suddenly aware that her own hero had switched his attention to another girl. It was the press officer, whose inviting shape was garnished with red hair and an inviting smile. The smile stayed in place as she expertly jotted down a few notes.

'So you saw this Donald Blake on one of his school visits?'

Dave Quinnan went over it for the umpteenth time. He pretended to be bored with the story by now; but really he had got it off pat, and enjoyed hearing the commendable truth about himself yet again. How he had noticed the red dog, the man's mascot. Such an unassuming man, so easygoing with kids. Or so it seemed. Only a police officer must always be alert, and PC Quinnan had been alert. How he did a bit of

9

checking back at the station, and how one thing led to another until they pulled the weird old blighter in and he coughed.

'No problem,' he said airily.

And no mention of the fact that Sergeant Penny had been the one who actually tracked Blake down and did the pulling in.

'It must be a great feeling.' The girl fluttered sandy eyelashes at him. 'Knowing you're responsible for having a monster like that put away.'

'Yeah, a bit of a high spot, obviously.'

'And what exactly would you say this commendation means to you?'

It was a relief to let himself be himself again, just for a moment. Grinning, he said: 'Insurance, isn't it? Makes it harder for them to give you the sack.'

It was unfortunate that Brownlow should have overheard the remark as he was making his way towards the group, anxious to be in the picture the photographer was about to take. It was also not to his taste that Mrs Quinnan should, at the last moment, put her arm companionably round his waist.

'A nice friendly group,' said the photographer, inviting a nice friendly crop of smiles.

PC Tony Stamp felt far from friendly towards the Sun Hill hero of the day. They often made up a patrol together, and were supposed to be mates. But right now Dave Quinnan did seem to be pushing his luck. He had not indicated that he would be off all day – and he owed Stamp a tenner. Typical. First to the bar every time, but not always the first to get his hand in his pocket. He needed to get his priorities right: like spending his own money when the occasion called for it.

Stamp glowered as he drove past the end of the shopping mall and around the corner on their drearily familiar route into the first of four housing estates on this patrol. You could never be sure which of the four might explode into violence, today or tomorrow or any other day. The tower blocks loomed above the car like solid, lumpy pylons which no one had thought to join up with cables. The clusters of four-storey buildings in between had been designed by some idealistic architect to alleviate the alien harshness of the towers, but simply looked cowed by them.

'Sierra One from Sierra Oscar.' Sergeant Peters' voice crackled out of the radio. 'Receiving, over . . . ?'

Cathy Marshall leaned forward. 'Receiving.'

'Disturbance at Abelman House. Fourth floor. Reported by a Mrs Curtis, number 422.'

'On our way. ETA two minutes.'

Stamp was in no mood for this. 'Two minutes? Who's driving, you or me?'

'Down the end' – she was unperturbed by his snarl – 'and do a right.'

He would have liked to do exactly the opposite, just to show her who was in charge. But in fact this was exactly the quickest and shortest way to Abelman House. Gritting his teeth, he accelerated to the corner, swung round, and could at any rate congratulate himself on having cut half a minute off her estimate.

They pounded up the concrete steps past a garish flowering of graffiti, and emerged on to the fourth-floor balcony. It was a sunny day, but there was a fractious wind cutting across their faces. With it came a rise and fall of voices, a yell and a screech, a pause, then two voices shouting wildly at each other.

An elderly middle-aged woman in a shapeless brown frock was waiting close to the stairwell.

'Mrs Curtis?' asked Cathy Marshall.

The woman nodded and jerkily indicated a door further along the balcony. 'It's been getting worse all week.'

Stamp didn't fancy this. 'Look, love, if it's just a domestic – '

'I know they've had a bad time.' She was not going to let him brush her complaint aside that easily. 'But one of them's

11

going to end up doing something really stupid. And there's a baby in there.'

Reluctantly Stamp approached the flat. As Cathy followed him there was a crash from inside. It sounded as if something had been thrown. Then there was a woman's scream: not of fear, but wild abuse. 'Bastard!'

Cathy Marshall said: 'What's their name?'

Mrs Curtis looked mildly surprised, as if they ought to have known this. 'Butler.'

After peering through the glass panel in the door, Cathy stooped to rattle the letterbox. 'Mrs Butler?'

An inner door slammed violently. Before she could call again, a shape blurred across the glass panel and the front door was yanked open. A woman in her late twenties stormed out, pulling a leather jacket over her low-cut orange blouse. She paid no attention to the two police officers, and had marched past them before either could protest. There was another slam of a door from inside, and a man of about her own age came out in a similar rush. He could have been good-looking, but was already going to seed. He brandished a lager can, which proved to be only half empty when he hurled it after his wife. Lager sprayed over Stamp's shoulder. He was fond of the stuff, but not in that way.

'Hey, cool it.' He caught Butler's arm. The man fought back. Cathy was about to pursue Mrs Butler when Stamp, shoving the man heavily against the balcony rail, said: 'Leave her, Cath.'

'Yeah, leave her.' Butler subsided as quickly as he had erupted, and let himself lean over the rail beside Stamp. 'She's not worth it.'

Stamp pushed his chin aggressively forward. 'So what's your problem, pal?'

'Me? Nothing. Everything's terrific.'

Cathy said: 'The lady along there said there's a baby indoors. Is it all right?'

'She's fine, yeah.'

12

'Can we come in and look?'

'I said she's fine.'

'And we'd still like a look,' said Stamp heavily. 'Any objections?'

Butler gave him a mock salute. 'Whatever you say.' He glanced at Stamp's shoulder. 'Number 595. I collect police numbers. Haven't got many.'

'Just show us the baby, please, sir.'

The child proved to be not a baby but a three-year old. 'Her name's Jemma,' said Butler offhandedly as he opened a bedroom door and stood back to let them look in. The little girl was bent over a couple of rather scruffy soft toys which might once have resembled animals. The carpet was threadbare, and there were yellowing stains on the walls and along the window-ledge. 'I take good care of Jemma.' Butler closed the door and wandered aimlessly into the living-room, which looked even more shabby and unkempt than the child's bedroom.

'Fine,' said Cathy Marshall, preparing to wrap it up and lead the way out.

Butler shook his head, smiling faintly. 'You don't know who we are, do you?' Now he was staring at her shoulder, too. 'You don't know, do you, 487? But we're famous.' Loudly, as if talking to the mentally deficient, he said: 'Butler.'

The penny dropped. 'Graeme . . . ?' Graeme Butler had been one of the children murdered by that man who for so long had been welcomed into schools and been so sentimental about his huge toy dog.

'Right! Our son was strangled by a lunatic. Remember? Of course, that was months ago now and you've managed to forget the lot. You're such busy, busy people, aren't you? You've got shoplifters to nick and parking on yellow lines and all those loads of lost dogs and stuff to sort out. *We* only lost a kid. And after a while we were solved and written off. So it's all neat and tidy and all right for you lot, isn't it?'

He swung his arm wildly, knocking a seaside souvenir off

13

the narrow mantelpiece. Then, unable to look any longer at the two uniformed officers, he sank on to the sofa and plunged his head into his hands.

Cathy gave a meaning little nod, indicating that Tony Stamp should stay where he was. She went into the poky little kitchen, which would have looked intolerably cramped even if it had been tidy – which it wasn't. She found a tin of instant coffee and three mugs, one of them badly chipped. The kettle was surprisingly new, one of the tall efficient ones: perhaps a Christmas present, or an essential replacement for an old-fashioned one which the Butlers had managed to burn out.

When she got back to the living-room, Stamp was standing awkwardly above the dejected Butler, who was making an effort to control himself and rub away tears or bleariness from his eyes.

Cathy put a mug on the low table by the sofa. 'I wasn't really involved in the murder inquiry myself,' she said tentatively. 'Not after the initial search.'

'Lucky you.'

'I mean, I'm sorry if you feel you've been neglected.'

All at once he was quite calm, looking at her with something between pity and contempt. 'Number 340. Another one for my collection of numbers. He came round. Brought back Graeme's clothes. In a plastic bag. "Here y'are, mate. We've finished with these. Happy birthday." Just like that.' He pushed himself up and went to a large sideboard too big for the room, probably taken from his or his wife's parents at the time of moving in. Opening one of the doors, he pulled out a plastic bag bulging with clothes, a pair of trainers, and a couple of photographs of a fair-haired eight-year-old boy. 'That's Graeme as far as you lot are concerned. All packaged up. All there is of him.'

She wanted to tell him about Quinnan's quick thinking, and how it had led them to Blake; how, if it hadn't been for Quinnan, maybe there would have been other children, others like Graeme and like Jennie Price. But he was beyond thinking

14

about other kids. Not callous: just numbed, and doomed to stay that way for months and years to come . . . maybe for a lifetime.

'We couldn't get his body.' He nursed the plastic bag, rocking very slightly to and fro. 'Not for weeks. It was like he didn't belong to us no more. None of our business. No visits, no information, nothing.' An edge of anger came into his voice. 'We only found out you'd caught the slime who did it by reading about it in the paper.'

'I'm sorry. It shouldn't have happened like that. The system . . .'

'What system?' he exploded. 'Lose someone in a mass wipe-out, then there's a system. A train crash or something big enough, and they swarm all over you. But you try having your son murdered. It's bloody lonely.' His fist clenched and his knuckles squeaked against the plastic. 'I even had to play detective to find out when the remand hearing was. And queue up to get in. To see the man who did it. I sat next to his daughter.'

Stamp sipped at his coffee and wanted to be anywhere but here. It was a relief when his radio came alive. 'Sierra Oscar to 595, receiving, over . . . ?'

'Receiving.'

'Can you state your position please, 595.'

'We're still at 420 Abelman House. Confirmed as a domestic. No offence disclosed. Over.'

'Can we expect you back on patrol shortly?' asked Peters in his characteristically light, sarcastic tone.

'Yes, sarge.' Stamp, all too ready to be off and out of this place, glanced meaningly at Cathy Marshall. 'Any minute now.'

Cathy was still studying Butler. 'The trouble between you and your wife . . . I mean, you didn't seem on the best of terms when we arrived. Were you arguing about something in particular?'

'We always used to row about Graeme. Old habits die hard.'

15

'You mean you still argue about Graeme? In what way?'

'Like whether we should leave his bed alone or sell it.'

'You want to keep it?'

'If that's all right with you.' He was glaring at her. 'It might not fit in a plastic bag.'

Stamp said: 'Look, it's high time we – '

'One thing. Denise can look after herself. You've got no worries there, officer.'

'You haven't had much support from the neighbours?'

'What, that nosey cow next door? She's a ghoul.'

'Nobody on the other side?'

'Squatters. And next to them is the heavy music. And after that they don't speak English. We're quite a little community up here.'

'You don't go to work, Mr Butler?' If he had to be kept standing here, Stamp had no intention of trying Cathy's pleasant, sympathetic act.

'Not since Graeme had his neck wrung, no.' Butler looked down at the label attached to the bag. 'Sorry. Property Number 2476 to you. Can I put him back on the shelf now? Got to keep the place tidy.'

As the man was stooping in front of the sideboard again and tugging feebly at the door catch, Stamp jerked his head at Cathy. They had wasted enough time here.

As they left the living-room a key rattled in the front door lock and it was pushed open. Mrs Butler came back in, loosening her leather jacket and preparing to toss it wherever it might fall. She pushed past them without a glance, headed straight for the television set in the living-room and switched it on.

Her husband closed the sideboard door..

'Back already?'

She threw the two police officers a hostile glance. 'What are they doing here? Looking for stolen?'

'They're concerned. About us. The old cow rang them. Not enough marital bliss.'

16

Mrs Butler turned up the volume of the television full blast and slumped down on the couch.

Butler looked as if he was going to say something to Stamp, but decided it was not worth it. He joined them in the doorway, ready to see them out.

Cathy looked dubiously back into the room. 'You're happy for us to go, Mrs Butler?'

The woman waved dismissively without even looking round.

At the front door Cathy said: 'Look, Mr Butler, I know someone should have said this to you before, but there are victim support organizations we'll be glad to put you in touch with.'

'Oh, we've had a visit.'

'But I thought you said – '

'I don't count voluntary workers who do it just for the kicks.'

'I'm sure that's not the way they – '

'That guy in a woolly jumper telling me to talk to him about pain? I told him to stick it where the monkey puts his nuts.' As she tried to interrupt, he raged on: 'I don't want sympathy, right? I don't want some prat I've never met before sitting in there nodding at me. All I wanted was to be treated like I still had an interest in *my* son.' He thrust his face close to hers. 'Okay? Thanks for calling.'

The moment she and Stamp were out on the balcony, the door was slammed behind them.

Good riddance, thought Stamp. He had really had a bellyful of folk like that. They ought to get off their backsides and make an effort to get on with life. There was no way of helping them. Give them the earth and they'd still bleat. If they had taken better care of the kid, maybe he would still be alive. A mega guilt complex, that was all they were suffering from.

As he reached the stairwell, Cathy caught up with him. He could feel she was still seething with some guilt of her own, or guilt on behalf of the whole flaming Force. 'Graeme's

17

clothes,' she said bitterly. 'Someone should have asked if they even wanted them back.'

Should have done? Stamp's lip curled. Procedures were always breaking down, all the time. That was why Chief Inspector Conway was always marching round with his Book 40, which he preferred to call his little squib book, dishing out rockets.

'Anyway,' he said, 'count me out of the lectures, right? I wasn't the one who stuck that plastic bag in Butler's hands. Hero Quinnan did.'

He led the way down the stairs.

'I suppose,' she cried from behind, 'you'd have stuffed it through the letter-box.'

This was too much. Just too bloody much. Stamp came to a halt and waited for her to reach him. 'Listen. I was the one who found Graeme Butler's body. You forgotten that? I trod on it on Canley Fields. And I was first on the scene when Jennie Price was found. In a plastic sack. I didn't sleep for a week. So don't pigeonhole me as a callous bastard.'

They went back to the car in a grim, throbbing silence.

PC Dave Quinnan left the Area Headquarters with some regret. It was a new experience to have senior officers making a fuss of him, having their pictures taken with him as if he were some special kind of visiting celebrity, and boosting his image with Suzanne. He had a feeling that within moments of his getting back to Sun Hill everything would get back to normal. Still, it had been good while it lasted.

He could tell that Chief Superintendent Brownlow now wanted them off the premises and away. Politely moving them down the steps, he was only half listening to Mrs Quinnan holding forth.

'Even as a toddler he was very quick-witted. Well, you have to be when you're the youngest of five.'

'Yes, I'm sure.' Before she could say any more, he offered

18

her son another handshake. 'Well, congratulations again, Quinnan.'

'Thank you, sir.'

'Early turn in the morning?'

There was no misunderstanding the implications behind that. Back to normal with a vengeance.

'Can we give you a lift?' Mrs Quinnan was reluctant to part with Brownlow. 'We've got a cab coming.'

'That's very kind, but I have my car.'

Mrs Quinnan watched him go, and squeezed her son's arm. 'It's been a gorgeous afternoon, David. What a pity Marcie couldn't come.'

Quinnan looked daggers at her. Suzanne, her pouting smile fading, frowned at him suspiciously.

'Who's Marcie?'

Feeling far from capable of coping efficiently and heroically with that question, Dave Quinnan was relieved to see a cab nosing its way round the corner. He hurried off ahead of the two women to meet it.

Two

Sergeant Tom Penny said: 'I bet he's the one who gets his photo in the paper.'

It was not until he had got up from his lonely table and was walking back towards the custody area that Sergeant Cryer joined him. Bob Cryer felt an obscure need to try and haul Penny out of his depression, without feeling that Penny particularly deserved to be hauled out. But they had been involved together in so many things over the years that the effort had to be made. Provided it didn't last too long.

'They all get their pictures in the paper,' he said soothingly.

'But Quinnan will be in front, flashing that smarmy grin at me.'

'I'll say this for you, Tom: you do know how to take things personally.'

'I think I'm entitled. I should have been up there as well as Quinnan. I was the one who found Blake in that park and persuaded him to give himself up. I interviewed him because he wouldn't talk to anyone else but me. I deserve the Award of the Strong Stomach for that alone.'

Cryer had to admit the truth of this. The Chief Superintendent could well have recommended both Sergeant Penny and PC Quinnan. Penny would forever be irked by it. His own opinion of himself was a very favourable one, if a bit misguided. When there had been that bit of trouble between him and his wife a couple of years back, and Bob Cryer had acted as a carefully-treading go-between, Tom Penny remained convinced that none of the fault was really his. If he had started drinking too much and kept up the habit, then somebody else had to be to blame. When somebody took the mickey out of him, he reacted with venomous hostility. Yet when he was in a black mood his own tongue was capable, just for the sheer sake of it, of scorching his colleagues and, most derisively, the men on the beat. And it was par for the course that when he genuinely deserved a recommendation, he should be passed over. Cryer knew uneasily why Brownlow had preferred the bumptious young Quinnan. Dave Quinnan, for all his cockiness, had potential. Tom Penny had none left. He had been around too long, stuck in the same groove and beginning to rasp against the sides of it.

Warily Cryer said: 'Tom, it's all over and done with, months ago. Does it matter? A DAC's commendation . . . I mean, after all . . .'

'Is a mark of recognition. Why Quinnan and not me?' On the edge of the custody area Penny gripped Cryer's shoulder. 'Come on – why?'

Cryer was alarmed by Penny's intensity. 'Look, I know you were disappointed at the time. But it shouldn't be gnawing away at you like this, mate. It's not healthy. Forget it.'

They went on into the charge room, to find Chief Inspector Conway sitting at Penny's desk with his precious Book 40 open at his left hand. Cryer slackened his pace rather than become involved in whatever creeping criticism Conway might be planning. He knew that predatory expression all too well.

Penny stopped dead. His voice was controlled, unexpectedly mild. 'Checking up on me, sir?'

'I'm checking up on everyone, Tom. And I'm not best pleased with what I've found elsewhere.'

'I trust you'll find the custody records in order, though.'

'Up to a point, yes.' Conway's cold fish eyes rose in a pallid, accusing gaze. 'Except for this matter of a certain Mr Paterson.'

'Richard Paterson,' Penny recited, 'bailed on the eighth, sir.'

'I know. So why haven't we got shot of his property?'

Conway consulted his troublesome little book. 'This is the third time I've asked and it's still not been actioned. Where's the arresting officer?'

With the greatest restraint Penny said: 'PC Quinnan is at the official commendation ceremony, sir.'

'Oh.' Conway got the message. 'Yes. Um, well. If he doesn't clear it tomorrow, he'll have an official reprimand to go on his file as well.' He got up and stumped past them. 'You sergeants have got to screw down on these procedures. Nicking people's not enough.'

'No, sir,' said Cryer quickly, before Penny could come out with whatever was brewing in his mind.

It did not take long to froth out. The moment Conway had left the charge room, Penny's precarious self-control deserted him. He lashed out and swept the custody records off his desk. 'That bloody Quinnan.'

'Easy, Tom.'

'Easy? He's up the road taking tea with the Queen. I'm here being made to look a prat because of his laziness.'

'I'll speak to him first thing tomorrow.'

'Oh, sure, you speak to him. Like you always do. The strokes you let him get away with, I think you must be having it off with his sister.'

Cryer was on the verge of losing his temper just as stupidly. Instinctively, he grabbed Penny by the collar and swung him round, then shook him and let him fall half into the chair, half against the desk. 'You're loopy. I really think you're going loopy.'

Penny bent down to retrieve the papers he had scattered across the floor. He pretended to be preoccupied with them for a moment, picking up pages and reshuffling them, then looked up with a twitching right eye and a trembling lower lip. The drooping pouches of skin under his eyes had become greyer and puffier these last few months.

'I'd rather be loopy,' he said, 'than a grotty little ratbag.

22

Commendation? It's farcical. I don't know how you can look me in the face.'

'Not many people want to nowadays, I'll agree with you there.'

'Why don't you come clean?' Penny was shouting now. 'You recommended Quinnan, didn't you? Brownlow asked for your twopennorth and you gave it him. I know bloody well you did. To hell with the twenty-year man, let the young smart-Alick have the bloody glory.'

'All right.' Bob Cryer found he was shouting back. 'All right, I recommended Quinnan. For his quick thinking. Spotting what we'd all been looking for, just when we most needed it. Using his initiative. When did you last use initiative? Except to get yourself out of the mire or drop someone else in it. Eh? Because unfortunately they don't give commendations for nitpicking. Or for bloody-mindedness. Or for being a 24-carat pain in the arse. Because that's what I think you are, Tom.' He drew a deep breath. 'And I'm your friend; so you can judge for yourself what everyone else thinks.'

At last Tom Penny was reduced to speechlessness. Angry as much with himself as with his target, Cryer snatched up a ballpoint from the desk and thrust it under Penny's nose. 'Here. Your biro needs sharpening.'

Before things could get even worse he stamped out towards the front office. Cathy Marshall met him with an account of her visit with Stamp to the Butlers' flat. It was obvious that it had upset her, and she was still upset, complaining about Sun Hill's heartlessness in the matter of the dead boy's clothes. As bad as Tom Penny – brooding over might-have-beens or ought-not-to-have-beens.

Cryer struggled to remember details, and then dismissed them. You could not forever be looking back at possible errors of judgement; least of all when they were not really your entire responsibility. He had not been personally responsible for the coroner's office, or the CPS – or the Home Office, come to that. All he could vaguely recall was that Dave Quinnan had taken Graeme's clothes back because CID had thought it would be a good idea. Quinnan had been involved in the case, and maybe the Butlers would be interested in what he had to say.

From what WPC Marshall had to report, the Butlers seemed to have been far from interested, at the time or later. They hadn't wanted to hear and had no intention of listening to anything ever again.

The sooner Marshall and Stamp got out on patrol again and found something fresh to occupy them, the better.

Tony Stamp was looking intolerably smug as Cathy slid into the car beside him. He had been waiting for her with quite some anticipation.

'Guess what?'

'Go on. Surprise me.'

'He's got form.'

'Who?'

'Butler,' said Stamp with relish. 'I've checked.'

She was a very pretty girl, with a smooth complexion and appealing grey eyes. But they looked far from appealing right at this moment. 'What did you do that for?'

'Because I knew in my bones he would have.'

Sod Dave Quinnan and his instinct and all that garbage. Stamp prided himself that his own nose for a suspect smell was as sensitive as anyone's, and better than most. Butler's whole attitude had given him away. It came as no surprise at all to find that he had three convictions for theft under his belt. And on top of that, his wife had been done as well – for shoplifting.

'So he can't feel grief,' said Cathy, turning away as if she no longer cared to look at him. 'He stole a packet of fags when he was eighteen.'

'Oh, come off it. Cath, we caught the murderer. Justice has been done. We don't owe these layabouts anything. If they can't help each other – '

24

'It's because they're slag,' she finished for him. 'Right? Well, the Prices aren't slag. Jennie Price's parents: they were a decent, happy family. And d'you know what's happened? I've done some checking, too. They've split up. Their house is up for sale. More wonderful aftercare.'

Stamp started the engine and revved up to a snarl. He still could not see that what went wrong with the Butlers or the Prices was any fault of his. Or of Sun Hill in general. People had lost their kids. Murdered. Gone. Bloody dreadful, all right. He would not forget in a hurry stumbling on that corpse or finding the second one, and the state it was in. But the kids were gone and there was no way they could ever be brought back. Even if the parents wanted help, what good could the police do on top of what they had already achieved?

'Can you resurrect children?' he demanded. 'No, you can't. All you can do is make coffee.'

He drove off on to the waiting streets and whatever else they might have to chuck up today.

He did not have long to wait. Again it was Sergeant Peters, and again it was Abelman House. Domestic disturbance. Only this time the call was from Mrs Butler herself, and a 999 call at that.

'So,' said Peters, 'can you straighten them out a bit better this time, please.'

Stamp shot Cathy Marshall an accusing glance. 'We'll be up and down there like yoyos now they've latched on to your indulgent ear.'

She remained silent as they approached the estate. This time there was nobody waiting at the top of four flights. Mrs Butler was at the foot of the stairwell, without her jacket and clutching her left arm with her right hand.

'Don't hurry, will you?' She had the strength to be aggressive, anyway, when Stamp was hardly out of the car.

He studied her without enthusiasm. Whatever the story was, he was inclined to disbelieve it before she had even started telling it. 'What's the problem now?'

25

'He's off his chump.' She turned her arm to show a shallow gash, oozing blood very slowly on to the palm of her hand. 'Went for me with a bread knife.'

'Why'd he do that, then?'

'How should I know? I told you, he's flipped.'

'Still up there?'

'Of course he's bloody up there.'

Cathy Marshall was already heading doggedly to the foot of the stairs as if to pre-empt anything Stamp might have in mind. He hurried to overtake her, passing her on the second landing and reaching the Butlers' front door a good few steps in front. There was no way he was going to play this one tactfully. That had been tried earlier, against his better judgement. Now it was going to be for real.

He rattled the letterbox. 'Mr Butler?' He gave it ten seconds, then yelled: 'Mr Butler!'

There was no reply. He was rather glad. It gave him the excuse to work off some steam by drawing his truncheon, smashing the glass panel, and putting his hand through to open the door.

Mrs Butler, reaching the balcony well behind them, let out a whimper of protest. 'I've got a key here.'

'Go steady,' said Cathy in an undertone as Stamp shouldered the door open and hurried along the passage.

The living-room door was ajar. He was conscious that Cathy, behind him, was opening the child's bedroom door and looking apprehensively in. She seemed to be reassured, closing the door again and coming close behind him.

'Is she all right?' whimpered Mrs Butler from the front door. 'Jemma? Is she – '

'Why the sudden interest in Jemma?' came a bellow from the kitchen. 'Part of the deal, is it?'

Stamp kept his truncheon firmly gripped in his right hand as he advanced on the kitchen. Inside, Butler was standing tense and wild-eyed with his back to the sink. One hand gripped the edge of the sink so that his knuckles were dead

26

white. Beside him on the draining-board was a bread knife, and fragments of smashed crockery lay on the floor at his feet.

'All right, pal?' asked Stamp warily.

'Get that bitch out.'

'It's you they're getting out.' Mrs Butler pushed her way close to Stamp's left shoulder. 'They're locking you up.'

'So you can have all the blood money?'

'It ain't blood money,' she shrieked at him.

'How much you selling our Graeme for? Eh? Fifty grand, is it?'

'My conscience is clear, so don't you –'

'You ain't got no conscience. Never have had.'

Stamp held out a restraining arm to keep Mrs Butler from hurling herself back into the fray against her husband.

'I was a good mother to that boy,' she howled, 'no matter what they say. The papers wouldn't want the story if they thought otherwise.'

'They want dirt and blood, that's what. And you're a slag.'

'What harm can it do Graeme now?' Her tone had changed to a self-pitying whine. Stamp sensed that it was more for his and Cathy's benefit than for her husband's. 'Tell me that. Why should we stay in this dump for ever? Why should Jemma? Eh? You're so wonderful, are you? What did you do for Graeme – what did you ever do except give him a slap when he nicked your lager? You ignored him half the time, and the other half you were legless.'

'You lying cow.'

Butler snatched up the bread knife and lunged in her direction. Stamp parried it with his truncheon, got an armhold on Butler, and with another twist sent the knife flying to the far corner of the kitchen. Cathy made a grab at Mrs Butler, but not in time to stop her throwing herself at her husband now that he was firmly restrained. She began screeching abuse in his face. 'No good you trying to take it out on me. Too bloody

27

late. My conscience is clear, which is more than anyone could say for yours.'

Stamp dragged Butler unceremoniously out of the kitchen. Before his wife could pursue him, Cathy Marshall caught her arm to hold her back.

Mrs Butler turned to her, suddenly pleading, woman-to-woman stuff. 'My conscience *is* clear,' she whinged, her self-pity turning to self-righteousness. 'I mean, it ain't blood money. You can't call it that. Like the guy from the paper said to me, maybe it can do some good. As a warning to people who read it.' When she realized that the policewoman's expression was one of unyielding disapproval, she added defiantly: 'Graeme's dead. You have to take what you can get in this life.'

Sergeant Penny looked across the charge room desk at Alan Butler, flanked by PCs Stamp and Stringer. Butler did not return his gaze but stared sullenly at his feet.

'You understand why you've been arrested, Mr Butler? We can't just shrug our shoulders at the use of a knife. If your wife decides to press the matter, we're looking at a charge of grievous bodily harm. It's fortunate for you that the officer intervened, otherwise it could have been attempted murder.'

Butler slowly and wearily raised his head, and shrugged. 'Thanks for the information . . . 54.'

He was led away. He had not asked to see a solicitor, nor made any attempt to talk himself out of what had happened. There was no real need for two officers to accompany him in case of trouble. He simply plodded into the custody area, along the corridor, and into the end cell.

When Penny checked him through the wicket before going off duty, Butler was sitting on the bench with his elbows on his knees, his hands clasped, staring at his feet again.

In the sergeants' locker room Bob Cryer was changing into his tweed jacket and trousers. He looked round, about to

28

speak. Penny veered away, hoping to get away out of here without having to make meaningless conversation.

But Cryer said: 'How's Butler?'

'Probably planning a good cry later tonight. Still, now he's in the system good and proper he'll get some help, won't he? Like Donald Blake.'

Then Cryer said what he had been dreading. 'Coming over the pub, then?'

Coming over the pub? To watch Quinnan flaunt his commendation certificate, listen to the cheap jokes and envious congratulations, to be patronized, or worse still tactfully ignored . . .

'You must be joking.'

'My treat.'

'I'll buy my own, thanks. And not in *The Freemasons*, either.'

'Still Dave Quinnan?'

Penny was not going to bother answering that one.

Cryer sighed. 'You're not hurting anyone except yourself, you know. Is it asking so much to be a little bit magnanimous, just this once?'

'I can be magnanimous. But I don't like pretending.' Penny crashed back the door of his locker. 'I don't fit in here any more,' he said tightly. 'Not with you or anyone else. I'm out of step.'

'Tom – '

'So I'll drink where I like. Where it suits me, and nobody else. And you can piss off and get pissed being matey with the lads.'

He grabbed his jacket, tugged it half on, and blundered out before Bob Cryer could get any more stupid remarks in.

There was a hell of a row coming from the pub as he passed it, swelling briefly as someone opened the door and went in. He wondered if it would have been as boisterous and congenial if he had been the one to get the award – the award that, God knows, was his due. He looked at his watch. A quarter past ten. And Quinnan was on early turn tomorrow.

Let him come in weary and bleary, and he'd soon find out how long the prestige of that bit of parchment could last.

There was another pub three blocks away where they did not know Penny or any of the rest of the Sun Hill officers. It was just that bit too far from the nick for them to bother. Though by now the regulars must be getting to know him by sight, anyway. He was making his way here more and more frequently, on his own, and taking a double scotch to the awkward corner near the door to the gents' lavatory, where only one person could squeeze in against the tiny shelf. Men going out to the lavatory glanced at him occasionally; some were by now nodding half recognition; but nobody spoke to him, and he never spoke to anyone but the barmaid.

Although a jukebox was pounding out and the place was packed, his corner was empty as usual. He stood at the bar long enough to down a whisky in three gulps, then took a refill over to the shelf.

Three

It was never easy to decide which was worse: getting up around dawn and arriving on a bleak morning for the early relief; or coming off night relief at six o'clock weary after a dull or troublesome night. Either way the hours made it difficult to contemplate any ordinary kind of daytime activity in between working and sleeping. And then when you were switched on to the late shift that left only the morning for shopping, home life, or the social round – a time when most people did not go in much for the social round.

Human beings, Reg Hollis had once observed after reading a medical pamphlet which someone had been rash enough to leave in his way, were not programmed for shift work. You couldn't fool their bio-rhythms. Some of the men managed to adjust over the years. Sergeant Alec Peters quite enjoyed the changeover period when, once every few weeks, he could be at home for several hours during the early part of the day. It was his favourite time to do the garden: the neighbours were out at work, so he did not have to listen to a load of advice. Others admitted that there were dangers of being taken by wives to buy furniture, chair covers, or rolls of wallpaper. The thing to do then was to ensure you were on an awkward relief when the time came to hang that wallpaper.

The women officers would have agreed with Hollis about the bio-rhythms, on top of a lot of other things. There really was no way round it. If you found a man with a normal job, he would soon get fed up with you being on shifts. And if you found one who was on shifts himself, the two of you might never meet. 'You want a bloke who does absolutely

31

nothing,' June Ackland had once commented. Somehow that would not do, either. In their job they had seen too many examples of what happened in relationships where the man hung around at home with time on his hands and nothing to occupy those hands. Not just the resentful unemployed, either. So life went on, and the unsocial hours went on in their different patterns, and there were times when it seemed there was little in life but plodding the beat, shopping at odd times and in odd places, washing your smalls, wondering why there was never anything interesting on the telly when you were off duty, and tumbling wearily into bed – alone.

Of course there were some people at Sun Hill who had the privilege of following a civilized timetable. Chief Superintendent Brownlow and Chief Inspector Conway kept office hours. CID were officially on a nine-to-five shift except when there was a panic on, and even then the additional hours could be virtually brought to a halt in the middle of an inquiry: in these cost-cutting times, it was difficult to get extensive overtime authorized.

The CID had other advantages of which the uniformed reliefs were jealously aware. If they were missing for a few hours, it could be assumed that they were on a special line of inquiry, or that they had tacit approval for taking time off in lieu of some spell of productive overtime.

Which was why, to her surprise, June Ackland found Detective Chief Inspector Wray one day suggesting that they should have lunch together. He had clearly worked out an equation in which the hour of her coming off late shift and having sufficient time to smarten herself up by one o'clock tied in neatly with his own tour of duty.

Only perhaps it was not, honestly, to her surprise. Several times she had seen him looking at her with a disturbing speculation in his eyes when they passed in the corridor, and he had twice congratulated her on a couple of not very remarkable collars in shopping precinct punch-ups. Being glanced at meaningfully was one of the daily hazards for a

32

WPC, often accompanied outdoors by obscene suggestions, and indoors by sniggers or, in the case of DI Burnside, blatantly crude jokes. But Gordon Wray was no Frank Burnside. His invitation, when it came, was quiet and courteous, and on the face of it innocuous. June knew that if she had turned the idea down in the same tone of voice there would have been no immediate argument.

Yet she had a feeling that he would simply bide his time, continue studying her, and try again later when he thought the moment was ripe.

She tried to pretend to herself that it was a matter of Sun Hill procedure. A frank discussion, maybe, on better liaison between uniformed branch and CID. But that would surely have been out of order. He would have had to approach Conway or Monroe first – and Monroe only after getting Conway's permission to do so – for any formal or even informal analysis of what was going wrong, or right, or whatever.

In any case, if there was to be a discussion on Force matters, it could perfectly well take place in the nick itself. You did not arrange a so-called working lunch at the expensive restaurant and carvery of the *Hunting Lodge* on the remotest outskirts of the manor. If she had any sense, she told herself, she would politely turn down the invitation.

But she was curious about Wray's motives. And she could look after herself well enough. That, too, was what she told herself as she left Sun Hill on night duty before the date they had fixed. Tony Stamp was on patrol with her, indulging in his usual line of chatting her up, but without any real intensity. She tried to keep her mind on the job and Wray well to the back of her mind. To some extent she succeeded: otherwise she would probably have failed to notice the humped shape in the shadow of a jumble of boxes and black sacks awaiting collection when morning came.

It was the shape of a middle-aged man. The smell might have been him or some rotting material in the boxes. He moaned as Stamp tried to heave him to his feet, and then

33

went slack as if all he wanted in this world was to sag to the pavement again and go to sleep. In the sodium glow of the street lights he did not look too scruffy; but neither did he look like a tolerably well-to-do citizen who just happened for once to have had one too many.

June radioed for an ambulance. A drunk tottering along the far side of the street tried to focus on them as they waited, but found the effort too much and was in imminent danger of finding himself crumpled up against a similar heap of rubbish.

The man snuffed it before reaching hospital.

That was the only incident of the entire night; which inevitably allowed the thought of Wray to creep back into June's mind. What on earth was she expecting to come of it? He was a married man, that she knew. And she wasn't even sure she liked him. Yet every time he glanced at her she was in some way drawn to return the glance.

Well, she would find out just over twelve hours from now. And – silently she said it again – she knew how to look after herself. Wray himself, she remembered as if it was somehow a perfect excuse, had on two occasions congratulated her on just that.

DI Frank Burnside was in expansive mood. He had arrived this morning without any good reason for finding life cheerful, but the news on his desk had been good and showed signs of getting better. All that was needed now was confirmation from Tosh Lines, who sat holding the phone, waiting for a call to be put through.

'Just ask about the preliminary results,' said Burnside. 'No need to mention my name.' He was aware of a primly reproachful look from DS Greig. 'You just concentrate on your needlework, Jock. And don't worry, I'm not pulling any strokes.'

'Hello.' Tosh was through. 'Detective Constable Lines here, from Sun Hill. Do you have a a preliminary PM report on Lester Bromley, brought in dead this morning? That's

34

right . . . yes, I'll hold.' To Burnside it seemed an eternity as Tosh leaned back, waiting, and asked amiably: 'Did you know him, then, guv'nor?'

'Indeed I did. Don't say you've forgotten how intimately Lester Bromley and me were acquainted? In fact, according to Lester, I shoved his head down a carsie and pulled the handle. You can't get much closer than that.'

Greig glanced up again, with even more pronounced distaste.

Suddenly Lines was scribbling on his pad. Burnside tried to read the writing upside-down, but even the right way up Tosh's writing was not the most beautifully formed in the world.

Tosh thanked his informant and put the phone down.

'Well?' Burnside demanded.

Even when it came to reading his own writing Tosh was not too sure, and a lot less sure about the pronunciation. But the words were music in Burnside's ears. Lester Bromley had died of a coronary occlusion by atheroma: in other words, a heart attack – natural causes, no suspicious circumstances. Burnside had never wished Bromley a great deal of good in this world, but now he was prepared to be magnanimous and hope the miserable little rat had at any rate been out on the tiles last night and flaked out the way he himself would have wanted to.

'Right.' He slammed his hand down on Tosh's desk. 'This calls for a drink.'

Greig could restrain himself no longer. 'Guv'nor, if you'll excuse me saying so, this is a bit sick. I don't know what you had against this guy Bromley, but – '

'I think you've got it wrong way round, Al,' said Lines. 'It's just coming back to me. I get a sort of feeling it was Bromley who had it in for the guv'nor.'

Burnside slapped him on the back. 'Right you are, old son. I've had a complaint from Lester Bromley hanging over me for nearly three years. Assault, according to him. It slowed

35

down my promotion to DI. And maybe more than that. God knows how long the thing would have gone on before it was settled.'

Alastair Greig nodded reluctant understanding.

'So, my haggis-bashing friend,' Burnside continued jubilantly, 'it's a working lunch in the back room of the Constitutional Club. And I'm in the chair. And if you're a fully trustworthy member of my firm, you'll want to put a few wee drams under your kilt and look happy about it.'

That was an order. Greig recognized it, though looking far from happy at the prospect. Tosh Lines, on the other hand, appeared to have no reservations whatsoever.

Burnside could not stay still. There was someone else who had to share in the gladsome tidings. He made for DCI Wray's door and tapped on it just as Wray was finishing a phone conversation.

'So I'll pick you up at your place . . . Yes. 'Bye.' Wray sat back, grinning for a moment, then nodded at the DI. 'Frank?'

'Just a quickie, Gordon. You remember that complaint that's been outstanding against me? We discussed it when you took over here.'

'Sure.'

Burnside was still too buoyed up by the news to allow himself any snide remark about Wray maybe not being in that chair at all if Lester Bromley had kicked the bucket a bit sooner. 'Well, it's all over. Finito.'

'Complaint dropped?'

'Complainant dropped. Dead.'

'Well, that'll be a great weight off your mind, in career terms.'

'In respect of which, I was planning a little team-building exercise this lunchtime. Nothing silly, of course. Hoped you could join us.'

'No can do, Frank,' said Wray quickly. 'Got a . . . a working lunch.'

36

Burnside waited to be told if there was anything he ought to know. But Wray simply stared and waited for him to leave.

'Never mind,' he said at the door.

'But thanks for asking. My thoughts will be with you.'

On the whole Burnside was not too displeased. The party might well go with more of a swing without the DCI's somewhat patronizing presence. He wondered what the mysterious working lunch would be about; and was prepared to bet that it would be a hell of a lot less entertaining than his own little bash.

Someone who could be relied on to welcome the distribution of free booze would be Detective Sergeant Roach. But Ted Roach was already out with Viv Martella, and neither Greig nor Lines could offer any hint of when the two of them might be back. There had been some hasty phone conversation with someone called Johnny, and Greig remembered Ted putting on his tough 'You'd better be there, son, or else' act. Greig would of course remember that sort of thing. He was a great one for picking up the shreds of other people's conversations, was young Alastair.

There was surely a chance that Roach and Martella would be back in during the morning, or at least might phone in to report what the hell was occupying their time. But when time was running out and his thirst was beginning to increase beyond bounds, Burnside ordered Tosh Lines to scrawl a note telling the absentees where the rest of the team would be. Even in Tosh's handwriting, Ted could be relied on to interpret a message of that nature.

Just before one o'clock four of them duly adjourned down the road to the Constitutional Club: Burnside, Tosh Lines, Jimmy Carver, and Mike Dashwood. It was typical of Alastair Greig that he should want to go to the bog, and have a good wash and comb his hair before joining them.

Burnside tucked a twenty-pound note into the top pocket of the steward's jacket as they were ushered into the back room, and waited for the first batch of drinks to be set on the table before them. 'Oh, and there'll be a pint and a whisky chaser when our Scotch colleague arrives. They're hard men where he comes from.'

'Al Greig's not a drinking man, guv'nor,' Mike Dashwood protested.

'Long skinny geezers like him have hollow legs. It's well known.'

Jimmy Carver shook his head. 'I can't see it myself. Not Al.'

'Me neither,' said Tosh Lines. 'You need proper bulk to soak up the booze.' He sat back and patted his stomach complacently. Nobody could deny that he had all the necessary attributes.

Greig looked momentarily startled to find a pint tankard and a large measure of whisky in a glass when he arrived. But his quick glance of appraisal showed him from the others' faces that they were waiting for some reaction. Burnside had to admire the way he squashed any hint of reluctance and picked up the beer as if it was his normal lunchtime diet.

Carver, pleased at feeling himself so much an equal in this team, launched into a story about a club and a bouncer, and two police officers who had tripped over one another; and the fact that he had heard the story from Mike Dashwood in the first place, and Mike had heard it from the absent Ted Roach, spoiled nobody's mood of goodwill.

Before Greig could finish his drinks, the steward arrived with two replacements. 'And don't be so long with the next refills.' Burnside winked benevolently. Again Greig managed to suppress any sign of apprehension.

Burnside took a long draught of bitter, and felt as it went down that this wasn't such a ropey old world after all. But where the hell had Ted Roach got to? He had no idea what he was missing.

Ted Roach and Viv Martella had spent an earlier half-hour of the morning in Whippingham Park, where not so many weeks ago Tom Penny had recognized the sad, bewildered-looking child-killer and taken him back to Sun Hill. It had been a favourite place for the man to exercise his dog. It was still a favourite place for that sort of thing, as a babble of barking testified; not to mention the need to watch where you put your feet. Young mothers with prams clustered at the junction of gritty paths to exchange compliments about their children, comments about last night's telly, and lamentations about their husbands or lack of husbands.

Roach and Martella were not here to walk dogs or to make silly noises at babies. A casual observer might have sized them up as a rather scruffy, impatient-looking man using the open air to vent his feelings on a much more smartly dressed daughter – or maybe a much younger girlfriend who was about to ditch him. In fact they were both equally impatient; but Martella was better at not showing it than Roach. He would soon be in enough of a temper to spoil their contact when it was made, if it was not made pretty soon.

A grey minicab drew up near the park gate. For a moment it might have been any old cab, cruising for a fare and stopping so that the driver could have a sandwich or a smoke. But when the door opened and the driver got out, Roach touched Martella's arm.

'About time, too.'

Johnny Westlake spotted him, and took a short cut across the grass. He glared suspiciously at Martella.

'Who's she?'

'*She* is a police officer,' said Martella tartly, 'so mind your manners, mate.'

They began to walk slowly along the path, Johnny in between the other two. He was a short man with blackened teeth and a ferrety profile. His head hardly ever stayed still. He glanced from side to side, looked over his shoulder as if afraid someone might steal his cab, and then under a tree in case someone was watching. His voice was thin, with a perpetual whine.

'You never said you'd have no one with you.'

'You didn't ask,' said Roach. 'Now, what have you got for me?'

'It's going down today.'

'So you've kept saying, Johnny. We didn't come here just to hear you say it again.'

'Definitely today.' Johnny's head twitched to and fro. 'He's booked me for lunchtime.'

'All right. Where?'

'Well, I can't be one hundred per cent sure until I collect him. Might change his mind at the last minute.'

'That's a big load of use.'

'We could put a tail on this cab,' suggested Martella.

'No way. You don't know what Dobie's like. He's nervous as a cat, he'll know.'

'The fact is, Johnny boy,' said Roach heavily, 'a postcard from you after he's made the connection is not what I'm paying for. That's not service. All that bit about him changing his mind – d'you mean you do know really where he's set to go?'

'Since they've tarted it up he's done all his dealings at that place way over the far side of the flyover. What used to be the *Coach and Horses*. Now it calls itself the *Hunting Lodge*.'

'Going upmarket, our Dobie. And you think that's where he'll be?'

'Unless he – '

'Unless he changes his mind, yeah. All right. Look, that's where we'll go. So, if he *does* happen to want a change for once, just you find some way of getting to a phone and ringing the desk there, and ask for . . . let's see. Mr Ransome sound convincing? Ask for Mr Ransome, and I'll come running.'

Johnny Westlake nodded jerkily. He stopped in his tracks, nodded again, and then turned to scurry off towards the gates. Roach glumly watched him go. He was a poor hope, but he was all they had got. So many things might go wrong. Especially where Dobie was concerned. Dobie was indeed known for being nervous, and was quite capable of changing his arrangements because of some last-minute alarm, or some twitch of a hunch. He had bought himself a Ferrari Testarossa out of his profits on dealing dope, but would never drive himself when he was making a connection. He was forever scared that the black rats would spot-check him, or a rival firm rip him off. So he made a practice of hiring Johnny's minicab; and, true to his cautious, apprehensive nature, always booked well in advance to make sure there were no last-minute fluffs. He trusted Johnny. Which, thought Roach, showed that in some ways he was nowhere near cautious enough.

Martella said: 'Back to the nick for the time being, then?'

'Not likely. Having Wray or Burnside or both of 'em down our necks, wanting to know what's going on or shoving us out on some crusade of their own? I want this one wrapped up between us.' He looked down at his stained leather jacket. It was not the sort of attire for someone intending to lunch at a smart restaurant. 'Tell you what. I'll need to dig out my second-best suit. You can come back to my place while I change.'

'Your place? Mm. So long as you know you won't get any change out of *me*.'

'Pity. A long time since we had any good juicy gossip around the nick.'

'Gossip's fine,' said Martella, 'so long as I'm hearing it, not part of it.'

They left the park by the side entrance and walked down to where the CID car had been parked under a lime tree. It had not been the best place. A number of sticky leaves had smeared across the roof and bonnet.

Roach drove off. By a quarter to one they were rolling into the car park of the *Hunting Lodge*, the two of them looking as smart as most of the frequenters of the place, even if the car did not match up to the assembly of BMW's and Carltons.

Still, it was no worse than the minicab facing bonnet out-wards, close to the exit.

Johnny Westlake, slumped in the driving seat, saw them arrive and buried his face even more intently in his paper.

Well, at least the wheelman was here as predicted. Which meant that if there was no joy anywhere else, they ought to be able to pull Dobie in possession. Ted Roach wanted a lot more than that, though. They had sussed Dobie as a pusher quite some time since. The point was to collar the courier. Who, of course, they did not know from Adam. No description, not a whisper.

Well, life was full of little challenges. Roach got out of the car and was about to head for the entrance when he remembered the role he was playing. He walked round to Martella's side of the car, opened the door, and waited courteously for her to get out.

Gordon Wray held the door open for June Ackland, and locked it after she was out. For a moment she thought he was going to take her arm as they went towards the entrance, but instead they walked rather stiffly side by side.

'Used to know it when it was a quiet, run-of-the-mill sort of pub,' he said. 'Then last year they opened the restaurant, and did the whole place up. But it's not too flashy. Quite a decent lunch.'

'Do they know you here, then?' she asked warily.

He looked as if he had not considered this until this very moment. 'No, not so's it would be a problem.'

A problem. Why should there be any problem, anyway, in a straightforward working lunch? If that was what it was. And of course it couldn't be anything else.

June was not sure that her queasy stomach would stand up to whatever food she was offered.

'Would you like a drink in the bar, before we go in?' For someone usually so brusque and even downright bossy, he sounded uncertain of the next move.

42

'Not unless you do.'

'No, serious lunchtime drinking knocks me out these days.'

A girl at the reception desk checked their table booking and took their coats. June slipped the cloakroom tag into her handbag as they moved further and further into the unknown; though it all looked innocuous enough – a small but smart restaurant with a bar leading into it, a couple of bored but polite waiters, and a flood of daylight through generously high windows. Not what you would call an intimate place.

But when they sat down she could not resist studying the occupants of neighbouring tables over the top of her flashily embossed menu and saying: 'I suppose this is the sort of place where bosses bring their secretaries to play footsie under the table.'

Wray appeared to be taken off his guard, still unsure and defensive. 'That's a bit behind the times, June. A man in a restaurant with a woman doesn't have to be a boss seducing his work force. They could be two business people having a working lunch.'

'Like us.'

He said: 'Ready to order?'

They were halfway through a shrimp and avocado mousse as starters when a man was shown to a table laid for two. He ordered a large gin and tonic, and sat alone, not looking at the menu which had been laid open before him.

'All right,' said June. 'So all this lot are doing business. What about the guy on his own?'

'Maybe he's *minding* his business. Give it a rest, June, you're off duty.'

'I thought this was a working lunch?'

His grin was becoming a bit rueful. Maybe he wished he had never started this whole thing. When the main course, goujons of sole for her and an escalope cordon bleu for him, had been set before them, he made a great effort and started talking shop. Ostensibly it was all about Sun Hill CID and Uniform presenting a united front to the Beat Crime Coordinating Group, but without making it look as if they had been colluding behind the backs of the supposed coordinators. Basically it was a matter of collating the most trivial details of work on each of the reliefs – early, late and night – with the day-to-day analysis in depth of CID, and working out plans which would combine resources rather than dissipate them, as was so often the case nowadays because of interdepartmental rivalries and suspicions.

June could offer a number of illustrations of trivialities and cross purposes, and Wray listened and nodded. But there was an undercurrent which had nothing to do with what they were saying. Silently he was telling her something else; or asking her.

A woman brushed past their table, leaving a faint tinge of expensive perfume on the air. She was tall and had a long, haughty face with raven-dark hair swept tightly back, not a strand out of place. Her pearl-grey suit had an austerely high collar, and the dark scarf in the throat of her blouse was almost like a black tie on a white shirt. The man who had been sitting morosely alone rose to greet her, with just a brush of his lips on her cheek that hardly amounted to a kiss.

June realized that Wray had stopped in mid-sentence. He glanced at the woman, then edged his chair slightly to one side and kept his face turned away.

'Hello,' she said, glad of the chance to break the earnestness with a light-hearted remark. 'Your turn to be minding someone else's business. Someone you know?'

'Not socially, don't worry.'

'Police business?'

He looked down at his plate, still keeping his head at that awkward angle. 'When I was on the Drug Squad. Celia Caldwell. Intelligence said she was a courier, working out of Madrid, with cocaine from Venezuela. Later she's supposed to have switched to one-kilo shipments from Florida when the British crack habit got going.'

'Would she know you?'

'I've never pulled her, but I expect they studied our photos like we studied theirs.'

Perhaps this was the key for the end of any personal aspect of their lunch together. 'Do you need to do anything about her?'

'I'll let the squad know she was on the ground. But it's no crime to have lunch.'

No crime. Of course not. June said: 'Did you tell any of your colleagues that you were bringing me to this restaurant?'

'Er . . . well, no.'

'No, and I didn't tell anyone on the relief. Doesn't that say something?'

He forced a smile. 'It says we both know what police stations are like for gossip.'

Viv Martella could tell that Ted Roach was coming dangerously close to the boil. Nothing was going quite their way today, and Ted was blaming himself – which always made him tetchy and liable to fly catastrophically off the handle at some ticklish moment.

They had settled themselves in the bar a few feet from their target, Nigel Dobie, who was perched on a bar stool doing the *Times* crossword. On the floor at his feet was a black briefcase. It was all Roach and Martella could do not to stare greedily at it. Then, just as they had ordered a scotch and a diet coke, a waiter had come through from the restaurant and indicated that Mr Dobie's table was ready. Through the door from the bar into the restaurant they watched him settle and order another drink; and watched as the waiter took the briefcase and returned with a cloakroom tag.

Now what?

They needed to be sitting at a table just as close as they could get. But when Roach approached the receptionist, she declared with such a nice, insincere smile that all the tables were booked. This was something he had not taken into consideration; and Roach was not a man to take kindly to his own mistakes.

Martella watched him turn on the charm, and could tell it had no chance of working. 'I realize it's ridiculously short notice, but you see it's my new secretary's birthday, and she's a very shy girl, and I didn't even find out about it until late this morning.'

She simpered and fluttered her eyelashes in what she was sure was a dismally unconvincing impersonation of an office junior. The receptionist spared her a sceptical glance, and repeated:

'We are fully booked.'

Roach waved a pleading hand, not disguising the folded ten-pound note between his fingers. 'What about cancellations?'

The woman smiled with her teeth but not her eyes. 'I can recommend the bar meals.'

They felt even more frustrated when a smartly-dressed woman in grey walked in, handed over a black brief-case, collected a cloakroom ticket, and strode confidently through to join Dobie at his table. She was gone before either of them had even glimpsed her face, and her chair was situated so that she was almost entirely hidden behind a column. There was nothing for it. They would have to order a bar snack and sit in a corner from which they could keep an eye on the restaurant door and the main exit.

Of course they could flash their warrant cards and march in. But then what? If the woman with Dobie was really his connection, they would hardly be passing plastic bags of coke across the table. Yet if neither Roach nor Martella could even eyeball that contact, this was really going to be a blowout. They had to get a look, but without showing size nine boots.

Martella might have guessed. Before she had finished her last mouthful of sausage and chips in a basket, Roach was saying: 'They're not going to make an obvious handover in public. Go and powder your nose.'

'I don't need to powder my nose.'

'The toilets,' he hissed with venomous impatience. 'They're the usual place for a quick switch, and that's what I think we're headed for. Just check 'em out. And see if there's a back door while you're at it – into a car park round the side, or anything of that kind.' He choked on a chip. 'We're not going to let them just walk out of here.'

She picked up her handbag and went towards the door at the end of the bar. Inside there were two other doors, one for ladies on the right, another for gentlemen on the left. An emergency exit at the end of the passage was slightly ajar. Martella peered out, to find herself in an alley between a line of outhouses and the door of the kitchen. Dustbins leaked discarded packets and unidentifiable chunks of meat.

The edge of the door had been spattered with grease. She turned back, and went into the ladies' toilet. She had just finished washing the dirt off her hands when the door opened and another woman came in. Martella stood aside to let her pass, then stared. She was not in uniform, but there was no mistaking her.

'June!'

'Bloody hell,' said June Ackland.

Four

They were looking helplessly at one another, each waiting for the other to make the first move. Finally Viv Martella took the plunge. 'What's going on? This is a CID job. Who told you lot?'

'I don't know anything about a job. I'm off duty, if you don't mind.'

'What are you sounding so ratty about?'

June had prickled with a sense of impending trouble right from the beginning of this lunchtime, but had not expected it to drop on her quite so soon. She braced herself. 'I'm here with Wray.'

'Ray who?'

'DCI Wray. Your boss. All right?'

'Whoops,' was the best Martella could offer.

'Exactly. I suppose you're here for Celia Caldwell.'

'Is that who . . . look, we're plotting up a pusher, Nigel Dobie.'

'Dark hair, round thirty, snappy dresser?'

'That's him.'

'And the bird he's having lunch with is Celia Caldwell, who's believed to be a coke courier.'

Martella beamed at her with mounting enthusiasm. 'Listen, you can help us out of the sediment on this one.'

June had been afraid of something on those lines. She nodded glumly, listened to Viv's quick concoction of ideas, agreed even more glumly, and made her way back to the table. From the far side of the room she could take in the general layout, and she was at once sure that Celia Caldwell had spotted and identified Gordon Wray. She was leaning well back in her chair, maybe getting a slant on him in one of the wall mirrors, and then leaning confidentially forwards to mutter something to Dobie.

June sat down opposite Wray, acting up with a smile as personal and affectionate as she could make it to lull the Caldwell woman's doubts. She was still beaming foolishly as she broke the news. 'I've just had the unexpected pleasure of meeting Viv Martella in the loo. It seems we're in the middle of a Sun Hill drug bust.'

'Who says so?' He had got the message, and managed to answer her smile with a positively amorous leer; but his voice was hard with rage.

'The guy your friend Caldwell's eating with is a local pusher, Nigel Dobie. Martella and Ted Roach have been keeping him under observation.'

'I am Sun Hill CID,' said Wray with a sunny calm which could have scorched Ted Roach's hair at a hundred paces. 'Why don't I know about it? I'm going to bite some people for this.'

'Well, the harm's done now, Gordon. We're conscripted. And the information is that Dobie's definitely scoring today. Right here, in front of our very eyes.'

'And where's Roach now?'

'Viv said they would go back to their car and wait.'

'Wait for what?'

'For us to act as beaters, I suppose you could say. Leaving it to us to decide how to get those two moving in the right direction.'

'Leaving it to us. How very polite of them.' Gordon Wray glared at his plate. Clearly he had lost whatever was left of his appetite. Risking a sidelong glance at Celia Caldwell, he caught her returning it and then looking away.

'My bet is that it's blown out. She's made me as the Old Bill.'

June pretended to laugh and tried to force a blush, as if he had just made some very forward suggestion – the sort of advance she had been expecting this very lunchtime until all this had cropped up. She discovered it was remarkably difficult to blush to order.

Celia Caldwell got up from her chair. She had glanced at Wray again and then at Dobie, and June had the idea she too was putting on an act. She was not saying goodbye but making the usual little grimaces and fluttering of the hands which indicated she was going to powder her nose.

Wray said in an undertone: 'Stick with her.'

June waited for Caldwell to disappear in the direction of the toilets, and then made similar phoney faces and sauntered as casually as possible in pursuit. If anybody wondered why she needed to go to the toilet again so soon after her recent visit, they'd just have to dream up some unsavoury notions about her bladder. As she went she was aware from the corner of her eye that Dobie was on his feet, moving towards the service door from the kitchen. And Wray was shoving back his chair and dashing across the restaurant without bothering to apologize to startled eaters.

At the last moment Celia Caldwell veered away from the door to the ladies' and headed for reception. In a couple of moments she was collecting her coat: just her coat, no case or package or anything else. She was very steady and calculating in her movements, showing no sign of panic. There was no quickening of the pace as she went down the three steps and across the car park to her Montego. June held back a few paces, not wanting to rush too obviously from the building.

Parked three slots away was the CID car. As Caldwell took the car keys from her handbag, Martella was swinging long, silk-clad legs out of the passenger seat and walking quickly across the space between them. Caldwell glanced back over her shoulder, and did a neat underhand throw of a little scrap of material into the shrubbery.

Martella showed her warrant card. 'Celia Caldwell? WDC Martella, Sun Hill. I'd like you to accompany me to the police station to assist with our enquiries into the sale of controlled substances.'

The woman tried to move past Martella, shrugging off the absurdity of the challenge. 'I'm sorry, I haven't the faintest idea what you're talking about.' She put the key in the door lock. 'If you'll excuse me, I have business to attend to.'

Martella grabbed her arm. 'Then I'm placing you under arrest. You do not have to say anything, but anything you do say will be noted down and may be used in evidence.'

'I'm aware of my rights.' The voice was steely and scornful, but there was a coarseness in it that belied the attempt at aristocratic disdain. 'I want to speak to my solicitor so that we can get this ludicrous mistake cleared up.'

Ackland emerged from the shrubbery, her dress slightly dishevelled and a scratch on her wrist from a spiky tendril of rose bush. She was holding a cloakroom tag.

'Yours, I think?'

'I have no comment to make until I've spoken to my solicitor.'

Gordon Wray approached from the hotel. Only he wasn't Gordon any longer, but DCI Wray. He had Dobie in tow, and a stain all down Dobie's right trouser leg suggested that a bit of a scrimmage in the kitchen had damaged not only the suspect but some preparations for a lavish Knickerbocker Glory. Wray nodded impersonal approval at June Ackland, so recently his lunch guest, and met Roach's questioning grin with stony self-control.

Celia Caldwell was standing erect beside the CID car with a watchful Martella beside her. Roach and Wray stood behind Dobie as he dug out cash, keys, a wallet and a credit card holder from his pockets and laid them on the bonnet of the car. The last thing to be reluctantly produced was a numbered cloakroom tag.

Roach beamed. 'Right, Mr Dobie, Miss Caldwell. Let's reclaim your baggage, shall we?'

June Ackland added herself to Viv Martella as the woman's

bodyguard. Dobie, after a moment's hesitation, followed sullenly. Ted Roach dropped back a few paces to have a word with his DCI.

He was enjoying this, soaking it for every flavour he could get. 'We can put Dobie on the sheet as my body, if it'll spare you embarrassment.'

'We'll do it by the book,' said Wray bleakly.

There was a lot of smoke in the air of the back room, and in spite of the steward's attentiveness an accumulation of empty glasses on the table.

Burnside looked over his men with mellow affection. They were all right really, all of them. Good lads. And it was a good day. It was rather like the day when his divorce came through – having the complaint off his plate at last. Complaints were all part of the job and you had to get used to them, but when they dragged on for years it could become a real sickener.

'It'll take a bit of getting used to,' he meditated aloud, 'not having Lester Bromley at the back of my mind.'

'Never mind, guv.' Alastair Greig suppressed a hiccup. 'You'll probably have a new complaint against you before long.'

That was not quite the reaction Burnside had been inviting. But he was in too good a mood to slap Greig down. One of the main treats of the lunchtime had been watching the po-faced lad getting pinker and pinker and hearing his voice getting more and more slurred. A few more large whiskies, and there was no telling what unguarded opinions might emerge.

'So there am I rolling on the ground,' Tosh Lines was holding forth, 'with this girl, and there's these navvies rushing towards us and I'm shouting, "It's all right, I'm the Old Bill, only I've left my warrant card in my other suit." ' He clutched himself, wincing at the memory. 'How I've got five children I'll never know.'

52

They had all heard it before, but they were all still in a mood for laughing anyway.

Still not a sign of Ted Roach. No matter how benevolent his mood, Burnside was going to ask some questions about that. What excuses was Ted going to offer for being out flannelling around the streets instead of being where the really serious action was?

Burnside looked at his watch. He didn't like what he saw; but there was no way of postponing the decision, and he was the one who had to pronounce it.

'Well, I'm for a Jimmy Riddle, then back to the grindstone.'

Jimmy Carver took the hint and rose unsteadily to his feet. 'I'll second that.'

Tosh Lines followed suit.

Alastair Greig attempted to get up beside them, but was finding some difficulty. Propped against the table, he glared at Mike Dashwood.

'I don't know how you cope with this lunchtime boozing, Mike. Sinking gin and tonics the way you do, like they were tap water.'

'Me? I've been drinking low calorie tonic water. I had a quiet word with the steward when we arrived. I don't want to turn into a pickled-livered tosspot like that lot.' Dashwood returned his sergeant's glare. '*I'm* surprised at *you*.'

They sorted themselves out and ambled back towards Sun Hill, Greig bringing up the rear. His first move when he got back to the office and found it hard to remain upright at his desk – or maybe it was the desk that refused to stay as still as he wanted – was to go off in search of a cup of coffee. He was so anxious to tip it down that it scorched his throat, without any immediate curative effect.

Tosh Lines came in cheerfully, slamming the door behind him with a thrust of his bottom, and dumping a plateful of hamburgers on the desk.

'Like a bit of ballast, sarge?'

Greig abandoned all hope and fled through the door, praying he could make it to the lavatories in time. Coming back fulfilled but feeble, he was still too shaky to be interested in the excitement created by Cathy Marshall and Ron Smollett in the doorway of the collator's room, busy disseminating information rather than collating it.

'Have you *heard* . . . ?'

On the table in the interview room were two brief-cases, already tagged as exhibits, and two cloakroom tokens. To one side of the table sat Celia Caldwell and her solicitor, a heavy-lidded Northern Irishman by the name of McCarthy. He was well acquainted with Detective Sergeant Roach and Detective Constable Martella facing him across the exhibits; but the acquaintanceship had never stood much chance of blossoming into friendship.

'Quite frankly,' he said, 'I see no reason for my client to be detained. You're talking about controlled substances. Nothing you've said so far connects my client with any such substances.'

'Let's go through it step by step,' said Roach amiably. 'When arrested, your client attempted to dispose of this numbered cloakroom ticket.' He jabbed a thumb towards the ticket, and then towards one of the cases. 'That token had been given in exchange for *this* . . . containing thirty thousand pounds in notes. Nigel Dobie was carrying a token which had been given in exchange for this other brief-case, containing a kilogram of cocaine. Miss Caldwell and Dobie had exchanged tokens – '

'That's pure speculation.'

'Miss Caldwell,' said Martella, 'why did you try to dispose of the cloakroom token?'

'You don't have to answer that,' said McCarthy sharply. 'There's no admission whatsoever that my client did any such thing.'

Celia Caldwell produced a condescending smile. 'Well, if it will help to get this unfortunate business settled, I'll explain.

54

While I was having lunch with Mr Dobie, I became aware that we were being watched. Since I had a large sum of money in my possession, I was alarmed by this. I decided to leave the restaurant and to get rid of the cloakroom token, since it would give access to the money to anyone who might attack me.'

'Whether or not that little bit is true,' said Roach, 'the money in question was payment for a consignment of drugs, wasn't it?'

'No. It was a cash payment which I'd collected from a business client – too late to get to the bank before my lunch appointment.'

'And would you mind telling me what sort of business client pays thirty thousand pounds . . . in cash?'

Caldwell looked quite cool and unflustered, at her haughtiest. 'The client of a discreet, exclusive, and resourceful prostitute. What else?'

'Thirty grand?' cried Roach. 'You don't expect me to believe that?'

McCarthy, equally incredulous for a moment, pulled himself together and tried to match his client's cool disdain. 'Sergeant Roach, it may be part of your duty to question my client's honesty. But to disparage the value of her professional assets takes you into the realm of oppressive interviewing.'

Martella stared fixedly at the exhibits on the table, aching with the desire to laugh.

When the interview was terminated and they were walking away down the corridor, Roach's confident bearing sagged. 'Odds are, Caldwell's gonna walk. We'll give it a spin, but I don't think we've got enough for a conviction.'

'But we've got Dobie bang to rights.'

'In possession. Sure.'

'Won't he grass on Caldwell?'

Roach shrugged. 'I'll give it my best shot, but he'd be a fool. Caldwell and her pals have got long memories and deep pockets. They'll probably look after him if he does his bird and keeps stum. And they'll definitely look after him if he doesn't.'

'The whole day could have been a bit of a blowout, then.'

'Oh, I don't know.' Roach cheered up again. 'There were compensations.'

They stopped at the foot of the stairs. 'Sarge, did you know about those two?'

'The police,' said Roach with a melodramatic throb, 'have eyes everywhere!'

They kept it impersonal for two days. There were brief formal reports to be added to the dossier on the Dobie and Caldwell case, though Wray shared Roach's doubts on the likelihood of them getting a conviction on Caldwell. He would have been particularly pleased to have fixed that woman, not just to show that he was better at the job than his old mates in the squad, but to get at least some compensation for a lunch date that had achieved nothing but the provocation of nudges and winks throughout the corridors of Sun Hill.

Better to play it very cool from now on. Wait a while. Or drop the whole silly idea altogether.

On the third afternoon their paths crossed in the station yard. It was touch and go whether they stopped, or just nodded non-committally and walked on.

They stopped.

'I'm sorry about that mess-up.'

'Couldn't be helped,' she said. 'What a tangled web, and all that.'

They were conscious of all the windows in the wall above. Their expressions, the exact reverse of the phoney loving act in the restaurant, were stiff and businesslike, as if they were conferring on a few last-minute queries about the case.

But he was saying: 'Next time I'll make sure . . .'

'Who says there's going to be a next time?'

'Isn't there?'

'We've got this far – '

56

'Not very far.'

'Far enough for everyone to think we're up to something.'

'So you think we might as well *be* up to something? Just like that?'

He was close to her, looking at her. Her hands clenched. He knew she was putting up only the feeblest kind of fight. She was going to give it a whirl: he could sense it.

'We'll have to fix some way of talking. Not out here, for God's sake. And not some flaming restaurant where Roach or Burnside are up to things I haven't been notified about. Or Conway is sending in his armies to round up a terrorist cell.'

'You're thinking of something like a candle-lit supper at my place, aren't you?' she said fatalistically.

He had not been thinking about it quite as clearly and definitely as that. Now he began to think about it, with a growing appetite.

Five

The rail of sweatshirts with gaudy motifs which usually added a splash of colour to the otherwise dingy row of shops had been taken inside this afternoon. The blast of taped music was at its usual shattering level, however, as the girl assistant unpacked boxes, hanging new shirts and jeans on the rail and adding some to the shelves and hangers along both sides of the congested space. She was a lightly coloured Trinidadian with a dark, sullen mouth. The name she had given to the policewoman called to the scene yesterday was Lagos: just the surname at first and then, as if it was something to be ashamed of, Charlene Lagos.

It looked like being all she was going to offer today, as well. Detective Constables Lines and Dashwood knew a stubborn face when they saw one, and guessed the reason for it. It wouldn't be the first time a key witness had refused to speak out because she was scared of the consequences. No, she hadn't seen the faces of the men who charged into the shop and left with armfuls of clothes. No, she hadn't seen the number of the car in which they raced off. Yes, she knew it would be a good thing if the police could catch them and make sure they were put away for a good long time, but she repeated that she could offer no positive identification. She tried to turn away and get on with her job of tidying up the shop and hanging replacement clothes as enticingly as possible.

Mike Dashwood kept his temper. 'Look, if we do get our hands on them and we can guarantee them being put out of harm's way for a long time, would you be willing to make a statement then?'

She rattled a sequence of hangers along a rail.

'You wouldn't be on your own,' Tosh Lines coaxed. 'This gang have done other shops. You know that. And we've got several people, some of 'em girls just like yourself, who've said they'll help when the time comes.'

'But not yet,' said Miss Lagos sceptically.

'Well, no. But the more supporting evidence we can build up, the more impressed the judge is gonna be. And the longer our friends get sent down for.'

Lines had edged along between the racks of clothes. The girl's doubting face appeared as a dark smear between a tasselled orange scarf and a sour green blouse. 'If you nick them,' she said grudgingly, 'I'll make a statement. Not otherwise.'

It was all they were going to get. They drove back to Sun Hill, knowing that Detective Inspector Burnside was not going to be pleased. Burnside always felt that if miracles could not be achieved by polite means, they ought to be beaten out of even the most uncooperative witnesses.

Swinging in between the gateposts of the station yard, Tosh nearly clipped one of them with his nearside wing. He had been distracted by the sight of a plump, smartly dressed woman walking towards the front entrance – a woman much darker and with fuller lips than the Miss Lagos they had just left, though apparently from the same part of the Caribbean. But Tosh knew better: he knew she had been born in West Ealing.

He swore. Mike Dashwood, jolted in his seat, swore even louder.

Tosh said: 'Did you recognize that?'

'I recognize a dicey near-miss when I see one.'

'That. *Her*. Delia French. It's true, then.'

'Oh, my God. What have we done to deserve this?'

It had been bad enough when the bumptious Delia had been a civilian, running the Sun Hill typing pool. They had

59

had to put up with a lot of lip, sometimes treating it as a great joke and sometimes as a bad joke. Delia had particularly had it in for the CID, whose erratic timetables and frequent demands for vast amounts of typing at unreasonably short notice made an orderly life very difficult. There had been sighs of relief when she left. Recently there had been renewed sighs – of apprehension, as word got round that Delia, for all her loudmouthed criticism of uniformed and plain-clothes officers alike, had been bitten with the desire to become a policewoman herself; and, worse still, that there was a likelihood of her being posted to Sun Hill.

And there she was, marching up the steps, looking pleased with herself. It could mean only one thing.

Lines and Dashwood made their way gloomily in from the yard as Delia dumped her large holdall on the floor and presented herself proudly at the front desk.

Steve Loxton came forward to deal with her. He had joined the Sun Hill team a good year or more after Delia had left, and looked her up and down without recognition and without any great enthusiasm. Being on duty in front office and dealing with a string of petty complaints and queries was never to his taste. He had joined the Force because he liked the uniform, liked the notion of belonging to some kind of élite, and fancied speeding around the scenery in the area car. His ambition was to be a PT17, a firearms officer; and that was not going to be furthered by frittering away his time indoors, coping with a succession of troublesome nobodies. Loxton was married, but there were whispers that he had a habit of treating his wife badly. Certainly he was brusque with the women officers at the nick, and did not much care for spending time in their company. A black woman had extra points against her in his view, though he would never have dared to say this out loud. There had, after all, been rather a lot of lectures on racial equality and caring, community policing.

'Yes, love?'

'Hi,' said Delia amiably.

He nodded towards her bag. 'Don't leave that on the floor, please. Security.'

Delia's grin faded. She picked up the bag and plonked it on the counter. In the doorway behind Loxton, Tosh nudged Dashwood as she opened the bag and pulled out a uniform tunic.

Loxton pored over it suspiciously. 'Where'd you find that?'

'It's mine. WPC Delia French. Okay?'

Before Loxton could gather his wits about him, WPC June Ackland brushed past Tosh Lines and opened the door beside the counter. 'Hi, Delia. Come through.'

Loxton made an effort. 'So you're the new plonk.' He held out a hand. 'Steve Loxton.'

'Hello, Steve.' Delia's smile was pure saccharine. 'I can tell you passed your interpersonal skills course.' She swept through.

'Been a few changes since you left us,' June commented.

'You mean CID have learnt to spell?'

'Nothing as big as that.'

Tosh Lines was blocking the way to the corridor and the WPC's locker room. 'Delia. So the rumour was true. What more could a man ask for on his birthday?'

Delia French looked him up and down, and let her gaze come to rest on his well-tended belly. 'A new body, maybe?' she suggested.

It really was his birthday, but clearly not one for special treats. Hard on the heels of Delia's withering remark came DI Burnside, jovial but ready to be just the opposite at the drop of a clanger.

'Any joy at the shop?'

'Same as all the rest. She'll give evidence, but only if we do the business first.'

'Better do it then, hadn't we?' said Burnside sourly. His eyes had darkened the way they always did when he was impatient for action but knew there was going to be difficulty getting the authority for it. 'Since we're pretty sure our old

61

friend Redpath is in this up to his elbows, and I'd lay you a hundred to one that house of his is more chocka with denim that Levi Strauss's wardrobe . . .' His mind was distracted for a moment as he gazed thoughtfully into the corridor along which French and Ackland had gone. 'Was that our Delia come back to be puppy-walked?'

'It was. It is.'

Burnside let out a thin whistle. 'Poor old Alec. He'd be safer with a rabid rottweiler.'

He went off in the opposite direction, up the stairs to see DCI Wray and urge him along to Chief Superintendent Brownlow's office. He could tell that Wray was doubtful about letting them go head down at Redpath; and if Wray was in one of his cold feet phases, Brownlow would be only too glad to go along with the feeblest of excuses. The Chief Super was a great one for not taking risks; and equally great, after an excess of caution had lost them a collar, in berating the whole team for slackness.

Burnside listened gloomily as his worst predictions began to come true.

'The thing is, sir' – Wray was putting on his most serious, responsible act – 'at this stage we can't really justify a raid on Redpath's premises. There's no concrete evidence.'

'Well, there's a lot of fear, isn't there?' said Burnside. '*I'd* be scared if half a dozen fifteen-stoners came steaming past me. And I'm not a slip of a shopgirl.'

Brownlow regarded him coolly. Oh, this had all the signs of a cold feet day, this one. 'No, you're not, Frank, and I'm not your fairy godmother. We are not going to rush blindly into anything without adequate prior surveillance. And surveillance comes expensive.'

'You're not going to knock it on the head before we've started, sir?'

'No, but you'll have to manage without the TSG. They're being deployed elsewhere.'

'So what happens if we're watching Redpath and he goes

62

on a shopping trip? We'll need to go in mob-handed if we're going to lift the lot of 'em.'

'Then you liaise with Inspector Monroe.'

That, thought Burnside, would be great fun. He tried not to let his feelings show in his face.

Brownlow's secretary put her head round the door from the outer office. 'Excuse me, sir. Delia French has arrived. Sergeant Peters asks if it's all right for her to come up ten minutes from now?'

The Chief Superintendent looked blankly at her. 'Who?'

Delia was hanging her civilian clothes in the locker as she put on her uniform, beaming more and more broadly as she did up each button. This was what she had been waiting for; what made that course and all that hard slogging worth while. The real thing at last.

'Got your handcuffs and hat?' asked June Ackland. 'Alec makes a principle of taking his probationers straight out from Day One, you know.'

'Oh, that's right. I remember.' Delia giggled. 'Alec Peters, teaching me all he knows – should be the shortest street duties course ever.'

'Now, Delia.' There was an unmistakable warning note in that voice. Delia tried to curb her bubbling exuberance. She must be careful not to put a foot wrong. Nothing must spoil her first day at Sun Hill. Or all the other days and weeks and months, for that matter.

She said: 'Well, anyway, what's the latest scandal?'

She thought June had stiffened for a moment, and then stifled some sort of reaction. But all she said was: 'Scandal? None, as far as I know.'

Delia sensed something; but this was no time to pursue it. And maybe things were harder to pin down when you were in uniform and not in the typing pool. Everyone had relied on her then for the latest dirt. Now the situation was different, and she would have to learn to play things differently.

She added another good resolve to her recent collection as she went off to see Sergeant Peters in the street duties course room.

Alec Peters at least had not changed. He still had that friendly, rubicund face, and a way of looking at you through his glasses with his head tilted slightly back. And she would have known that good-humoured voice anywhere.

'Hello, Delia. Great to have you back.' He sounded as if he meant it. Nodding at her uniform, he added: 'Suits you.'

'Thanks.'

'Take a seat.' He waved her towards a chair on one side of the table, with a ring binder lying on it. 'So. Street duties course. Over the next ten weeks I'll be showing you the ground, giving you a taste of the different shifts, introducing you to people you don't know, and places you'll need to know.' He opened the binder, settled his glasses more firmly on his nose, and perused the top sheet. 'Your first course at the Area Training Unit is the crime course. I see that begins on the third of next month.'

'D'you know' – she could not keep it back, could not help getting the smart remark in, just the way she had often done in the past – 'I was the only passer-out at Hendon last week who didn't get a visit from their upcoming street duties sergeant?'

Peters was still turning the pages of the binder. 'Yes, well, as you were the only one coming to Sun Hill, and you're already familiar with the station . . .' He shrugged.

Nor could she keep from insinuating some of the odd personal little things she remembered about him, just as she remembered them about everyone else on the strength. 'And you had a snooker match?'

That went home. He looked up, unamused and unexpectedly tough. 'No, I didn't. Look. Let's get off on the right foot, shall we . . . constable? When you ran the typing pool you could get away with a lot of cheek. To whoever you liked.

You don't have that luxury any more. You're a uniformed police officer. On probation.'

Delia gulped. 'Yes, sergeant.'

'You keep your mouth shut, and your eyes and ears open. Is that understood?'

She said with genuine fervour: 'Yes, sergeant.'

'Good.' He glanced at his watch. 'Right. Time for you to scamper upstairs and see the Chief Super. Then we'll get straight out on the streets.'

WPC Delia French, duly reprimanded and accepting it with a growing respect for Sergeant Peters, went obediently up to Chief Superintendent Brownlow's office. But when she looked at Brownlow she thought of some of the silly things that had come through the typing pool when his secretary, Marion, had been otherwise engaged or away on leave. And some of the Masonic giveaways in what he naïvely supposed to be unbreakably coded messages. It was difficult to take his pomposity seriously; but after that brusque warning from Sergeant Peters she forced herself to make a stern effort. At least he had had the manners to organize two cups of tea for them, though she had the impression that this had been a bit of a last-minute scurry.

Trying to get to grips with something he had not really boned up on, Brownlow asked a few polite questions, managed to sort out memories of her running the typing pool, and wondered what had brought her back here in such a different guise.

How did you explain to a man like Brownlow, who had forgotten what it was like to be a real policeman? He was an administrator now, high above the hurly-burly. He had found his way up the ladder, all right. So couldn't he see, without asking, what she was after as well? You were always looking to better yourself; to see what you could do. Delia had left the typing pool for a job in the City, thinking that was a step up. Public Relations: it had sounded so grand. But it turned out that she was expected to be just a glorified receptionist, so she thought to herself that she had already learned a lot better things than this, and it was time she applied them. On top of which, she wanted to make up for what her father had failed to achieve, coming so optimistically to this country and learning some hard facts the hard way.

'Y'know,' she beamed at Brownlow, letting herself rant on more than she had meant to, 'I kept saying to myself, come on Delia, you don't want to sit on your backside smiling at yuppies for the rest of your life. Damien, that's my little boy, he's big enough for me mum to cope with now when I'm not there, so I thought why not go for something different. Go for it. A challenge. So I applied. Didn't really expect to get to Hendon, but I did. Kept plugging away. And here I am, back where the real action is.'

Brownlow was clearly disconcerted by this wholehearted approach. 'Er . . . you asked for Sun Hill specifically?'

'Of course. But again I didn't expect to get it. Everything's worked out really well.'

He produced one of his routine smiles. 'Let's hope that continues, then. It's not an easy job, especially' – this was his frank, courageous line – 'for someone with a black skin. We have to accept that fact.'

'I've got no problem with my skin. If other people have, that's down to them. I intend to give this job one hundred per cent, and that's all there is to it.'

His smile was a lot warmer, almost approving. 'I'll warn the criminal fraternity accordingly.'

Delia felt she had carried it off rather well, and went down glowing with confidence to start her perambulations with Sergeant Peters.

For the first twenty minutes or so it was a dreamily unreal experience being out on these familiar streets in his company: familiar, yet now so subtly altered. She had done lunchtime shopping here many a time, and often exchanged a wave and a flippant remark with Sun Hill men on the beat or passing in a patrol car, half identifying with them or ignoring them, whichever way it suited her. Now she was one of them, and the streets and shops and passers-by were all changed – all, somehow, on the other side.

The other side of what? And whose side was she on now?

Surreptitiously she glanced at herself in a shop window, seeing the solid assurance of the uniform and the haziness of her own face; wondering what kind of impression she would make on other people.

'Caught you,' chuckled Peters, spotting what she was up to. 'How's it feel, then?'

'A bit weird, actually,' she confessed. 'Like everyone's looking at me.'

'I spent my first week thinking my flies were undone.' This was the relaxed, friendly Peters she knew best. 'Mind you, folk might look but you won't get many who speak. Don't let it put you off. Relentlessly cheerful, that's me.' He offered a smile to a lanky youth with a scrubbing-brush hair style, shrugged when it was not returned, and then led Delia towards a shop whose wares had been spilled out over trestles on the pavement because there was no space inside. 'Come on, let's say hello to Sunny. You'll have to get to know him sooner or later.'

The contents of the shop were as chaotic as the goods on the trestles outside. It was difficult to decide what Sonny Khokhar's special trade might be, unless he claimed to be London's leading specialist in unspecialized junk.

'Anything you need from time-expired yoghurt to perished knicker elastic,' said Peters loudly as they entered, 'he's your man. If you can find him.'

The jibe flushed out the proprietor. Cheerfully excitable, he fussed his way between two mounds of fruit juice cartons and what looked like a job lot of baked bean cans, tripping over an unopened box on the floor and spreading his arms wide.

'Alec, how you doing?' He stared with unabashed interest at Delia French. 'This your daughter? She's better-looking than you.'

67

Before Sergeant Peters had finished a brief introduction, Sunny Khokhar was already trying to sell her a pair of jeans.

Alec Peters shook his head. 'Expanding the clothing department, are we?' He winked at Delia. 'It's a hypermarket, really. Six foot square but a hypermarket. God help Marks and Sparks if he carries on this way.'

Sunny was dragging out garments from the heart of a teetering pile of goods. 'Men's, women's, you name it, we have it. Take a good look.'

He strewed several pairs of denim jeans across a mound of other clothes. Delia fingered a couple of them, holding them up to such light as managed to reach the back of the shop. They didn't look at all bad.

Peters was also examining a pair. He looked a lot less appreciative.

'Where'd you get these from then, Sunny?'

'From my supplier. Why?'

'And who might that be?'

'Well, this lot was . . . Hey.' Sunny took alarm. 'What's all this about? Something wrong with them?'

'I don't know. But our Tosh Lines might be able to shed some light on the matter. I'll just try and raise him. And hopefully put you in the clear.'

'Now, look – '

'Hold it, Sunny. I'm not saying they're nicked. And I'm not saying you know they're nicked. But I do need to settle a few little points.'

Sunny Khokhar launched into a tirade in some Asiatic language which meant nothing to Delia and less than nothing to Peters. After a moment the sergeant flapped a weary hand, trying to subdue the shopkeeper while he turned to his charge for the afternoon.

'Look, Delia, do you want to get out in the fresh air for a minute? I'll have to get through to Tosh and hang around till he arrives, just in case our emotional friend here tries to top himself with firelighters or something. Christen your pocket-book, eh? Go and check a few road funds. Just up to the junction and back.'

Delia was delighted with the chance of freedom to walk out on her own, watching the world without the sergeant at her elbow telling her what to look for.

She set a slow pace along the row of shops towards the minor crossroads. A mobile coffee stall was set on a patch of hard-beaten earth which might once have aspired to be a flowerbed. There was a row of parked cars along the gutter. Diligently she peered at each tax disc, and had a quick check of the rest of each vehicle for good measure. It was only when she reached the next to last in the row that she gleefully came across a disc that was a good two months out of date. She had begun noting down the details and the car registration number when there was a raucous shout from a few yards away.

She had come closer than she realized to the coffee stall. Five or six young men in their twenties, dressed in a mixture of frayed leather jackets, scruffy pullovers and deliberately torn jeans were drinking from Coke cans. An older man had brought his own can of beer with him. He shouted something indistinguishable but almost certainly obscene, and the others set up a chorus of catcalls.

Delia tapped the windscreen of the car. 'This belong to any of you?'

They shook their heads derisively. The older man put his thumb over the opening in his beer can, shook it, and directed spurts of beer all over his companions. They began to yell even more loudly in rowdy mock aggression.

'Could you just keep it down a bit, please?' said Delia as authoritatively as possible.

'Keep what down?'

'Can't even get it up.'

The older man spread his arms wide and began to sing at the top of his voice.

'That's it, Ringo – go on, let her have it.'

Delia took a step towards them. 'The noise, right? Keep the noise down.' She jerked a thumb at the man they called Ringo. 'Come on, pal, get yourself home.'

The babble broke out again. 'He ain't got no home . . . *you* go home . . .' And Ringo himself was jeering: 'Go on, get back up your tree.'

Delia went on pacing slowly closer to the group. She was getting scared but had no intention of stopping. She was in uniform. They had to do what she said. That was what the uniform was all about. 'I said keep the noise down.'

An unmarked transit van swung into a vacant slot between two cars. From the corner of her eye Delia could see it was parked at an awkward angle, with its offside rear wheel up on the pavement. But she had no time to go back and deal with that now. Ringo had gone down on his knees before her, raising his arms and bellowing even more loudly and less tunefully.

Delia raised her own voice. 'Look, if you don't all shut up I'm gonna start nicking people.'

She pointed her finger at the group. It was fatal. They wagged their own fingers and set up a caterwauling that made passers-by move well out to give them a wide berth and glare reproachfully at Delia.

'Go on, then,' Ringo implored: 'nick me, darling.'

Helplessly Delia tried to retract. 'I don't want to have to nick anyone, right? I'm just asking you to keep your voices down.'

Ringo stumbled to his feet, took her arm, and began pushing her back along the line of shop fronts. 'Station's this way. That I do know.'

'No. I don't *want* to arrest you!'

In the driving seat of the van Detective Constable Jim Carver was about to get out and head for Sonny Khokhar's mini-emporium when Tosh Lines said: 'Hey, hold it a minute.'

'What's wrong?'

'Look back there.' Tosh lifted the video camera from his lap and called over his shoulder into the back of the van.

'This has gotta be worth a bit of tape, hasn't it?'

Detective Sergeant Ted Roach looked out of one of the observation windows and began to chuckle wickedly. 'Has it just.' He took the camera from Tosh and focused it on Delia, who was struggling to stop herself being pushed backwards along the pavement. As it began recording he kept up a running commentary over his shoulder.

'Fancy her meeting Ringo on her first day out! Uhuh, watch it . . . he's gaining ground. No. She's holding her own. Better than holding *his*, anyway. A few feet . . . no, she's blocked him. Tug-of-war the other way round. Hold it.' He edged the camera round at an angle. 'I think she's nicked him. Or he's waiting to be nicked, anyway. Hands out for the cuffs – only she's not playing.'

Carver watched, spellbound, in his wing mirror.

'Oh, that's done it.' Ted Roach sounded disappointed. 'Here comes the Old Bill.'

The three of them craned to see what was happening. Alec Peters had emerged from Sunny's shop and was quickening his pace towards Ringo and Delia. One word from Peters was enough for Ringo. He gave a mocking little salute and scurried back to his mates by the coffee stall.

Now Jim Carver and Tosh Lines got reluctantly out of the van, and Ted Roach opened the rear doors.

'You all right, Delia?' Peters was saying. 'Just what's been going on?'

She was smoothing her uniform down, quivering with a mixture of rage, relief and apprehension.

Before she could answer, Tosh said: 'It's all right, Alec, we had her covered.'

Peters stared as Ted Roach dropped on to the pavement, still holding the video camera. Delia French was staring, too, not understanding. Peters all too clearly understood. He glared at Roach in genuine anger.

71

Ted Roach grinned. 'Camera drawn this morning on behalf of Detective Constable Lines. Official permission for him to take pictures of his celebration this evening and the wife and kids during birthday dinner tomorrow.'

'You'll need Cinemascope to get Tosh's family in,' growled Peters. 'And that's no excuse for – '

'Just wanted to check it was working properly.'

'And maybe now, if you can spare the time, you'll go and have a look at that gear in Sunny's supermart. Should be able to find a vanload there.'

Taking no chances, they did in fact make quite a lot of space in Sunny's shop, relieving him of several piles of denim clothing. Sunny himself followed them agitatedly to and fro, growing more voluble and less coherent by the second. The general gist of his lamentations seemed to be that this was the last time he would ask the police for help and probably the last time he would as much as speak to a police officer even if one happened to be run over in the gutter immediately outside his door.

Lines treated it all with beaming good humour. After all, it was his birthday, there would be drinks immediately after duty, a day off tomorrow to recuperate, birthday supper with the family, and at some stage in the proceedings a few minutes of good sport with that precious video. On top of which they had made what promised to be a useful haul, and maybe some words of commendation when the whole thing was wrapped up.

It was turning out quite a good day.

He waved amiably as Sergeant Peters and WPC French continued on their beat.

Delia suddenly had the first call on her radio. Tilting it with an eager but inexperienced hand she said: 'Er . . . 832 receiving.'

It was PC Garfield's voice at the other end. 'Will you be coming in for coffee soon, dear?'

'Tell him to get stuffed,' said Peters. When they had gone

a few more paces he added: 'I shouldn't have left you on your own. I'm sorry it ended in tears.'

'I'm not crying,' said Delia defiantly.

'No, good girl. But there's a lesson in it. A very important lesson, actually. Don't bark if you're not prepared to bite. You should have walked away from a situation like that.'

'And just let yobbos take the mick?'

'All they what is a reaction. Once you start arguing the toss, you've got nowhere to go, have you? You either end up arresting ten people for laughing, or more likely you get yourself hurt. Use your brain, right? It's the only one you'll get. And steer well clear of that drop-out Ringo in future.'

Delia nodded, chastened.

They paced along for another ten minutes while Peters indicated some traditional local trouble spots and explained the probable timing of that trouble. There was a so-called social club above a laundrette, run with precious little community spirit but plenty of the other sort of spirit. It was perfectly legal but had a nasty habit of chucking out its members around midnight, when they frequently threw up all over the highway or picked fights between here and the public garden beyond the bingo hall. 'A dump,' Peters summed it up. 'But never any trouble on the premises. Always outside. It's the open air seems to go to their heads.' Then there was this corner where the illicit street traders hoped for a brief profitable spell on Sunday mornings; the café where some constables out on patrol thought they had the right to while away fifteen or more minutes unnoticed over tea and bacon sandwiches – which, said Peters fiercely, they couldn't; and a sequence of shops, each of which had its own little dishonesties for which a regular quiet warning was better than a full-scale frontal assault.

A patrol car swerved in to the kerb beside them. Tony Stamp leaned out towards Delia and said very politely: 'Excuse me, constable. Anywhere round here I can get a cup of coffee?'

Peters bristled. As he went to stand by Stamp's open

73

window and launch into a lecture, Delia edged backwards. When Peters had finished and watched Stamp drive hastily off, he turned to find that she had disappeared. It was too much. On her first day out he had managed to lose WPC French again.

He sighed with relief as she emerged from a telephone box.

'Sorry, sarge. I just thought of something.'

'Try to think of things before you come out on duty. In this job we can do without too many distractions.'

'Yes, sarge.'

'Right.' He gave her an encouraging smile. 'Try again, shall we?'

'Sure.' She sounded very cheerful, and there was an odd little gleam of triumph in her eye.

Six

The video camera lay on the floor in the back of the van. Ted Roach, switching his bored gaze for a few moments from the outside world, patted the camera and allowed himself a little smirk.

Jimmy Carver had been munching a sandwich. Puffing a few crumbs away from his lips, he said: 'I don't go for that. Not on her first day.'

'Come on, Jim. Not as if we wound her up in the first place. Just an opportunity taken.'

Carver shook his head. 'And Tosh is going to show the video at the pub tonight? That's cruel, and you know it. And unprofessional. What if we missed Redpath while we were pratting about back there?'

'We were no more likely to miss him than we were while I waited for you to go to the toilet, wash your hands and find a clean hankie. And what's wrong with a bit of a wind-up, all of a sudden? You were happy enough to stitch up Cathy Marshall that time, way back.'

'That was different. She had it coming.'

'Yeah, and she's white, of course.'

'That's got nothing to do with it.'

'Oh yes, it has. Delia's one of your protected species. That's the way you see it, eh?'

'The way I see it,' said Carver heatedly, 'is that some folk want to get their own back on her just because she knew when to use a semi-colon and they didn't.'

'You've got a very short memory, mate. That girl made our

75

lives a misery. All that lip. Why's Tosh Lines got a complex about bad breath, for instance?'

'Because he's *got* bad breath.'

Roach grunted and returned to his vigil. It was just as well. He was in time to see three youths in their late teens emerging from the house under surveillance. Two were black, one white; and one black, the biggest of the trio, was Redpath himself. He was folding clothes-shop carrier bags and pushing them into his pockets.

Roach grabbed the camera and began filming through the observation point.

'You did change the tape?' asked Carver, worried.

'Just get yourself on the air and tell 'em the lads are on the move.'

Carver sprawled over towards the radio. 'Sierra Oscar from DC Carver.'

'Receiving.' It was George Garfield.

'Redpath and two others are heading in the direction of the High Road. Looks like a shopping trip. I'm following on foot. Could you notify DI Burnside, please.'

'Understood.'

'Thanks. Out.'

A moment later Carver was literally out, walking briskly along the opposite side of the road. He was in little danger of making himself conspicuous. There was the usual afternoon traffic of people going towards the shopping street or away from it, gossiping on the steps of the public library, enough to embrace his own movements but not too crowded to make his pursuit of the three youths difficult. In any case, the lanky Redpath towered head and shoulders above most of the passers-by.

In the High Road the trio slowed. Carver tensed. There were two likely targets within a couple of hundred yards. But instead of heading for the nearest clothes shop, a larger store than Sunny's or the other one which had been done last week, they went into a burger bar at the junction with Plover Street.

Carver looked into the window of a television rental shop across the street, getting a tolerable reflection of the front of the burger bar. It looked as if Redpath and his mates were only having a coffee. They were not intending to be in there long.

As he turned to look as casually as possible along the street, three other men sauntered into the bar and joined the three already there.

This looked like something real and big.

He edged into a doorway and bent his head over his radio, thankfully raising DI Burnside. Now the responsibility was the guv'nor's, and Carver could just visualize him, dashing off to raise uniformed back-up from Inspector Monroe – or liaising, as the Chief Super liked to put it – and arguing about the number of men who could be spared.

Now there was nothing to do but wait. He prayed the six men would not leave too soon, or make their following moves in too much of a rush. It was the sort of situation in which rivalries between CID and uniform branch were forgotten, and you were grateful for the sheer weight and solidity of the likes of Stringer and Quinnan.

Dave Quinnan stood back with an exaggeratedly polite bow as WPC June Ackland headed briskly for the liveried police carrier and climbed in. Her companion, Suzanne Ford, paused to return Quinnan's repeated bow with a pert grin.

He said in an undertone, mock serious: 'Whatever's slipped up? How come June's on this one?'

'Taking out the types that are too rough for the likes of you, I expect.'

'Wouldn't have thought the DCI would have sanctioned it. I mean, if *I* was over the side with a plonk, I'd do my best to keep her in good decorative order.'

WPC Ford abandoned her friendly, joshing attitude and favoured him with a glare of distaste as she followed June into the interior.

They were on their way.

DI Frank Burnside was not so much on edge as on his toes. Action was what he liked best: preferably when he was in charge and could deploy his forces the way he thought best. So he might have to carry the can for a failure. It was better than obeying someone else's orders and watching the whole operation being cocked up.

He set Tosh Lines and Mike Dashwood to stroll along the shopping street a careful distance behind the six men. From the back of the surveillance van he saw Jim Carver in a doorway, and directed Ted Roach at the wheel to pull in and pick him up. They wanted not the faintest chance of Redpath's little lot spotting Jim's face and wondering whether they had already seen it too often this afternoon. The van then slowed outside a delivery door between a pet shop and a Chinese takeaway, as if the driver had lost his way and was trying to pick out a name or number from one of the shop fronts.

Redpath stopped outside a downmarket clothes shop with a wide entrance and a well-spaced sequence of rails hung with jeans and sweatshirts inside. From the van Burnside could glimpse only Redpath's head, but Dashwood's voice came quietly into his radio. 'They're going in. Any minute now.'

Redpath had sauntered inside the shop on his own. Two others followed, taking their time, then the final three. Tosh Lines concentrated on a lurid pair of boxer shorts in the window, labelled with suggestive slogans.

The men inside tweaked clothes to one side and looked at the price tags. Redpath casually held up a shirt and put it casually back. The shop assistant, very young and very anxious to please the customer she was dealing with, smiled and went through the credit card routine at the till, and smiled and said 'Thank you, thanks, have a nice day' as the woman left.

The moment the customer was well away down the street, the thieves swung expertly into action. Redpath and three

78

others began snatching pairs of jeans from the rail and stuffing them into their plastic shopping bags while the other two stood between them and the petrified assistant. The girl made one attempt at a protest, but was immediately told to shut up. She looked at the faces of the two men guarding her; and shut up.

'Not exactly subtle, are they?' observed Dashwood, moving into position alongside Lines and rapping out details into his radio.

With their shopping bags bulging, the six men turned towards the doorway. Dashwood and Lines stepped smartly in front of them.

'No rush, lads,' said Lines. 'I think you've forgotten your receipt.' He flashed his warrant card. 'Police.'

Redpath, in the lead, hesitated only an instant. Then he dropped the two bags he was carrying, ducked his head, and charged straight into Lines. Tosh gasped as his built-in bumper of flesh took the impact. The two of them crashed out across the pavement, bringing down a middle-aged woman with a shopping trolley. Burnside and Carver flung themselves out of the van, with Roach hot on their heels, and at the same moment the liveried police van jarred to a halt and disgorged uniformed men and women to join in.

Dave Quinnan and June Ackland hauled Redpath off Lines, but the black youth's fingers were digging so deeply into Tosh's shirt that he had torn it almost in half. Quinnan was thrown backwards, and June Ackland was shrugged contemptuously to one side against the shop window. Redpath was away, scattering shoppers as he went.

Grimly Quinnan regained his balance, tottered a few steps, and then gave chase, with Phil Young racing to catch him up. Young was an insecure young man who aspired to the Stamp and Quinnan macho style but hadn't quite made it yet. Today might be his big chance.

Sergeant Peters had just pointed out the alley off a side street in which it was advisable to ignore a regular amount of snogging but important to watch out for drug addicts fumbling with their needles, when the familiar outline of a police carrier drew level with them. The horn tooted. Stringer leaned out of the cab. Before he could speak, Delia jerked her thumb back the way he had come and said cheerfully: 'Coffee stall's that way.'

Deflated, Stringer said: 'How about a lift instead?'

Peters anticipated Delia. 'Where you off to, then?'

'Inside Leg. Room for two more inside. On the way out, anyway. Might be loaded on the way back.'

Peters hesitated, then shook his head. 'Better not.'

Stringer drove off. Before Delia could ask what was behind the Inside Leg reference, Peters said: 'An anti-shoplifting job. That gang of hardnuts who just walk into shops and take what they want. They've done about ten grand's worth over the last few months.'

Delia felt her blood beginning to race. This was the way she had visualized real policing, instead of merely overseeing the typing pool and getting everything secondhand – and in deadly dull handwriting, at that. 'Well, couldn't we – '

'No,' said Peters, 'we couldn't. You've had enough naughties for one day.' At the end of the road he turned down a path beside a cluster of trim allotments, leading on into an even quieter back street. Evidently he was determined to keep them on a pedantically routine path, well out of the war zone.

There was so little to observe and so little to be explained down here that Delia found herself embarking on a family saga. About her father and his ten years as a bobby on the beat in Kingston before deciding to head for England and offer his services and depth of experience to the Metropolitan Police. It had been quite a blow when he discovered that there were only certain jobs which immigrants were allowed to do; and never mind those ten years in Kingston. 'You can't help wondering, y'know, would race be such a problem if they'd set about recruiting black bobbies way back in the fifties.'

Which was what she had tried to imply to Brownlow without being at all sure he was taking it in. And now she realized that Peters wasn't taking any of it in either, but looking at something way down the street.

He quickened his pace, crossed to the opposite pavement, and studied a pair of legs in grubby trousers and heavy brown boots but devoid of socks, sprawled beside a red Ford Fiesta. The rest of the man was half into the gutter, looking up and tapping the inside of the front wheel with a hammer.

Peters kicked the sole of one of the boots.

'Hello, Raymond.'

Delia wondered whether this was all being done to impress her with the sergeant's encyclopaedic knowledge of the manor and every resident in it. Look at me, he seemed to be saying, and get it into your head that it'll take you at least twenty years to learn what I know about all the ins and outs of this neighbourhood.

Only Peters was not showing off. His tone was light, but his stare was unblinking as he watched the man called Raymond squinting up and then nodding recognition.

'What'ya want?'

'What are you supposed to be doing?'

'Testing.'

'Testing what?'

'The car. I've tested them all.' Raymond waved complacently at the row of cars parked all the way down the slight slope, and made as if to resume tapping with the hammer.

'On your feet, please,' said Peters wearily.

Raymond shambled to his feet. His shirt was unbuttoned and overflowing the waistband of his trousers. He wore puce and lime-green braces, which rested on the extreme tips of his shoulders and appeared to be dragging his trousers sideways rather than supporting them. He smiled ingratiatingly at Delia. 'Test yours if you like.'

She wondered if he was genuinely simple-minded or if it was all a cunning act to mask some devious practices. His

81

smile did seem innocent enough. She kept quiet, waiting to latch on to Sergeant Peters' tone and treatment.

Peters had taken the hammer from Raymond's clutches, and stooped to pick up a pair of nail scissors from the gutter. 'Been testing the locks as well, have you?'

'No.'

'You sure?'

Raymond went on smirking at Delia French. Without warning he reached out and touched her, like a naughty child.

'That's enough of that,' said Peters. 'Where's Pauline?'

'Dunno.'

As Raymond made another dab at Delia, Peters caught his arm and turned him away along the street. Raymond went without protest, and Peters let go in order to fall back and let Delia catch up. 'Good as gold,' he murmured, 'when he's full of pills.' He turned the hammer over in his hand. 'Fortunately.'

'Aren't you going to nick him, then?'

'Do me a favour.'

She had hoped for some useful comments on the situation, but that was all she got.

Raymond, staggering slightly, looked back and leered at her. 'Do you fancy me?'

'No,' said Peters, 'she doesn't.'

It was true; but she would rather have been given the opportunity to answer on her own behalf.

Raymond seemed to expect little trouble from the police. He quite unfussily led them to his home. This might have been because he knew that Peters knew the address anyway; but Delia did not get the impression that any such logical throught processes would have guided the man in anything he did.

They reached a large Edwardian house which had seen better days. The lumpy patch of grass within rusted front gateposts quite devoid of gates had become the dumping ground for a shattered tricycle, several wooden boxes spilling out unidentifiable metal waste, and a scattering of bricks. It was one of those middle-class family houses which had long ago been split up for multi-occupancy, with a minimum of shared amenities.

Peters led the way up the cracked front steps and pressed one of the bells without bothering to check the card behind the stained plastic. Delia deduced that this was not by any means the first time he had been here.

'Council still cleaning up your flat, Raymond?'

Raymond shifted his weight from one foot to another. His remote, couldn't-care-less attitude deserted him. 'Hurry up! I need to go.'

Eyeing him with some concern, Peters pressed again. 'Do these bells work?'

'She must be in the garden.' Raymond came up to the door and began kicking and thumping it. 'Hurry up! I can't hold it much longer.'

Peters glanced at the passage between the house and its neighbour, divided only by the remains of a wooden fence which might once have been decked with roses. Dubiously he handed the hammer and nail scissors to Delia. 'Just keep your distance.' He hurried away round the side of the building.

Raymond wailed and began to beat frantically on the front door again.

It opened suddenly and a woman with straggly brown hair and a stained apron with an illegible pattern of London tourist sights reached out to haul him inside. As he lurched away down the corridor, she stared fiercely at Delia.

'Has he been having sex with you?'

'No. Honest.'

The woman snatched the hammer and scissors from her grasp and slammed the door shut. Delia turned back, taking a couple of hesitant steps back towards the street and wondering how long it would take Peters to reappear from the back of the house. He was a dogged type, tougher and more ploddingly determined than she would ever have guessed within the confines of Sun Hill station routine. As she reached the pavement she became aware of shouting in the distance, as if a peace demo had taken its usual turn for the worse. As it grew louder, she waited, unsure whether Sergeant Peters or an incipient riot would reach her first.

Peters had already started back when he heard the same shouting, drawing nearer. The alley behind the house had narrowed and led to a number of back gates which it was hard to allocate to specific houses. He tried one and found it locked; and the wall, more substantial than the side fence, was too high for him to see over. He had a feeling that if there still remained any outside lavatories behind these properties, it would by now be far too late for Raymond Kellow to have made his way there. He hoped for Raymond's sake and for Delia's that Mrs Kellow had admitted her husband in time.

As he returned to the passage beside the house, the shouting grew louder. He was puzzled by the resemblance of one voice to that of PC Philip Young, raised in what sounded like a rasping war-cry. There was a thump of running feet. All at once the unmistakable tall figure of Redpath exploded into the alleyway from a side path and came charging full pelt at him.

There was no time to escape, even if Peters had wanted to. He went down with a jarring pain as his left shoulder was bashed against the wall. He grabbed at Redpath's leg, but it was torn away and he got a hefty kick in the ribs for good measure.

Quinnan appeared in the distance. 'After him, sarge!'

Winded, Peters was incapable of dignified reply as Quinnan and Young pounded past him. He struggled up, watching the sharp left turn the two constables had to make in their pursuit. Obviously the alley looped back towards the road. Peters lurched back the way he had come. The short cut might enable him to outflank Redpath in the street.

His calculation had been correct. He reached the street as Redpath was halfway across, heading for another entry on the far side. But WPC French had got there first. She threw herself at his legs and brought him down in a spectacular rugger tackle. He lashed out violently, threshing from side to side and trying to shake her off. But Delia was holding on like a terrier. Peters dashed towards the two of them as Quinnan and Young panted out of the alley.

Redpath heaved himself up.

'Lie still,' screamed Delia, 'or I'll bite your ear off.'

Her ferocity was such that Redpath went limp for a moment.

It gave Quinnan and Young time to reach them and haul Redpath to his feet. Peters puffed his way to join them.

Crumpled in the gutter, Delia French beamed up at him. 'You'll be glad to know Raymond made it in time, sarge.'

He held out a hand to help her up.

Tosh Lines sat on the edge of his desk in the CID office stripped to the waist, sewing his torn shirt. Half an hour from now they were due across the road for the birthday booze-up, and he was still not finished. Typical of the way fate treated you. 'First clean shirt I've put on this year, and look what happens,' he grumbled.

'Would you like us to have a whip-round?' Mike Dashwood suggested. 'I expect Sunny's still open.'

'Na.' Tosh held up his shirt and inspected his handiwork with some pride. 'It'll do. It's only a birthday, not a funeral.'

'Oh, by the way – apologies for absence from June Ackland. She's had a busy day and, well, y'know, sorry and all that but she's got things to do.'

Tosh snorted. They all knew perfectly well who was doing what to whom. Mucking up a guy's marriage. Though June was hardly a vamp, and DCI Gordon Wray must have made the running. Still Tosh felt uneasy in the stomach about that sort of thing. Though plenty of things made his stomach uneasy nowadays. He must be careful not to have too many pints this evening and find himself with a hangover next morning, unable to appreciate his day off and the treats Maureen and the kids would have prepared for him.

Twelve years of marriage, and still only one wife – plus five kids. In his last nick he had been the only bloke in CID on his first wife. It still made him feel a bit like a virgin. But he wouldn't have had it any other way.

The shirt would do. It was time to get ready and go across to the *Freemason's Arms*.

In the corridor he passed Wray and Burnside. The DCI said: 'Oh, Tosh, how's the birthday boy?'

'Ready for the next fifty, thanks, guv.' He could not resist it. 'Coming across for a quick one?'

'Have to be a very quick one. You won't mind if I don't stay too long, will you?'

'Tosh'll understand,' Burnside broke in meaningly. 'I mean, he's like you – got a wife and family to go home to.'

Wray tried to look as if he was taking this remark at its face value, but the scattering of sandy freckles on his pale face seemed to glow a deeper russet. He spoke too bluffly. 'Right, Tosh, see you over there.'

As Tosh went downstairs he saw Sergeant Penny ahead of him, on his way out of the station. He was about to call out and remind him about the celebration; but the back of Tom Penny's neck made it somehow obvious that either he would fail to hear or would have to improvise some surly excuse. Celebrations were not in Penny's line.

The upstairs room of the pub looked overcrowded with so many Sun Hill personnel in civvies packed into it, and the fug they had already created spoke ill for any advertising campaign against the evils of smoking. Tosh was greeted with a roar of applause, a few bars of 'Happy birthday to you', and cries of 'No, that comes later'.

Several rows of chairs had been arranged in front of a television set and video recorder. Tosh grinned in anticipation. Then he was swamped with mates insisting on getting him a drink, thrusting a glass into his hand and ready with another before he had taken even two mouthfuls. A good job the missis had decided that, like the Queen, he was entitled to two birthdays: one today, and his official one tomorrow for the cakes and presents and all that.

Through the crush he saw Delia French come into the room, and elbowed his way through to greet her.

'Many happy returns, Tosh.'

'Thanks, love. Now come right in.' He escorted her towards the front row of chairs but kept her standing, with his arm companionably round her, trying to ignore Jim Carver's disapproving scowl.

'Ladies and gentlemen . . .'

The hubbub hardly slackened until Roach yelled: 'Best of order, please.'

Gradually voices faded away into an expectant hush.

Tosh Lines said: 'Ladies and gentlemen, can I just introduce the star of the show, without whom this evening's entertainment would not be possible. Will you welcome, please, Miss Delia French.'

There was an outburst of applause and whistles. Tosh directed Delia to a seat. When he was sure she was settled he picked up the video cassette from the top of the television and inserted it into the recorder. Right, this was it. Here we go. Light the blue touch paper and retire immediately. He pressed the play button and settled himself comfortably beside Delia.

She was smiling. You had to hand it to her. With a good idea of what was in store, she was behaving like a bloody good sport.

The recorder began to play.

Tosh and those in the know waited for Ringo to appear on screen, going down on his knees before Delia, and Delia fighting him off. He could guess at the sort of running commentary Quinnan or Garfield might feel inspired to contribute.

Something had gone wrong. Had there been something earlier on the tape which they had not noticed? A few minutes of leftover recording, or something? It was a bit of a letdown: expecting to see Delia and Ringo tussling it out on the pavement, the audience was presented instead with the picture of a white car drifting in towards a kerb that was certainly not within miles of the High Road.

The figure of a chubby man in a tatty mac got out of the car and began walking towards two obvious prostitutes in a doorway.

There was a murmur of recognition and then disbelief, followed by a swell of laughter. Tosh was the last one to realize whose that figure was. It was only when the camera caught him in full profile, with his stomach bulging out of the seedy mac, that he knew he was the one to be offered up as a treat to tonight's audience.

There was no soundtrack, which somehow made it all look worse. More ridiculous. Not that anyone would have heard a soundtrack: not with the hoots of laughter and ribald shouts, culminating in a wild roar as he and one of the girls went into the building and closed the door behind them.

Tosh twisted round in his chair. 'That was a serious operation.'

'Expect you needed one afterwards.'

'We got convictions out of that.'

'I'm not surprised,' bellowed Quinnan.

There was a brisk cut in the film to another street, another prostitute; but the same Lines, doggedly heading for her.

'He's at it again, look,' Quinnan went on. 'There's no holding him!'

Tosh's head was overwhelmed by the baying and laughing rolling over him from behind.

Delia French was leaning towards him. 'Happy birthday

from my old acquaintances at the Vice Squad. Their tape's much better than yours.'

She patted her bag. WPC French's first day in uniform at Sun Hill had been a day to remember.

Seven

Complaints about the dumping of rubbish generated a familiar headache in Sun Hill. As an irritant they took their place alongside reports of noise from ghetto-blasters, cars parked so that they blocked gates and paths, kids kicking footballs against shop windows, and women soliciting in back streets. You listened to the same old stories day after day, made notes, promised to do something as soon as you could get round to it, and got it all out of the way as quickly as possible – ready for the next moan.

PCs Young and Loxton, plodding on a dull beat at eight o'clock on a dull, drizzly Wednesday morning, would have welcomed some action to break the monotony. A peevish nightwatchman complaining about sacks of rubbish being dumped on the building site he was supposed to be guarding was not what they regarded as a welcome break. They picked their way over rubble which was almost an excuse for anyone to confuse the site with the council dump only half a mile down the road, and reluctantly inspected the bulging heap of black plastic.

'We're getting sick of this,' whined the watchman.

'Yes, well. We do have a lot of things to do.'

'The law's the law. I'm doing my job. Do yours.'

'If you were doing your job, mate, why didn't you see the stuff being dumped?'

'I did.'

'Then why didn't you stop it?'

Before the man could answer, Loxton let out a low whistle. He was stooping over one of the sacks, unknotting the top.

When it opened, a new video recorder tipped out. Behind it was a CD player.

He groped for his radio. 'Sierra Oscar . . .'

'It's not my place to get thumped stopping villains,' said the watchman. He held out a scrap of paper with a car registration number scribbled on it. 'Here you are, then. Get going on that.'

Loxton, through to CID, got going.

By the time DS Roach had reached his desk that morning, Tosh Lines had an early edition of interesting news waiting for him. Terry Jackson was at it again. Stolen goods ditched on a building site, car registration that tallied, rough description by nightwatchman not complete but emphasizing bushy eyebrows. And they had really thought Jackson was going straight this time. Ought to have known better.

Roach and Lines set off.

Tosh was a bit on the quiet side, suffering not from a hangover but from the surfeit of food he had shovelled into himself at his birthday dinner. The day off with the family seemed to have exhausted rather than invigorated him.

Roach was in no mood for light conversation, either. It was quite some time since he had last hammered at this front door. He had hoped then that it would in fact be the last time. It was a shabby but clean semi-detached council house, with a well-tended patch of front garden. The house and garden contrasted with the shoddiness to either side. You could really believe that the tenant had genuinely reformed and was using his energies to keep his wife and kids in decent style. It was a pity to break into that idyll; but it looked as if Terry Jackson himself was the one who had done the breaking.

Shena Jackson opened the door. She was too thin for beauty, or even for prettiness, but she had always been a sparky character, with pale eyes that could go the strangest shivering blue when she was angry. Ted Roach had always liked her, and been sorry for her, even when she was defiantly lying: usually lying to try and protect her unpredictable husband.

A girl of about eight years put her head out from behind her mother. She had Shena's pallid skin, but her eyes were as dark as her father's.

'Grown, hasn't she?' said Roach. He could not help feeling friendly towards the two of them. But he hadn't come here to be friendly. 'Is Terry in?'

'Yeah.' Automatically Shena stepped to one side to let him pass, then said: 'Hey, just a minute. He's going straight, you know.'

'So we've heard.' He nodded towards the door off the hallway. 'Through here?'

'Hang on.' She brushed past him and opened the door. 'Terry . . .'

Lines was on Roach's heels as they went into the sitting room. They were presented with a view of the back of Jackson's neck. He was slumped on the sofa in front of the television set, but the set was not switched on.

'You look tired, Terry.' Roach paced round him and sat on a chair close to the television, staring at Jackson's unshaven face and his reddened eyes. 'Doesn't change, does it?'

'What do you want, Roach?'

The detective sergeant looked away into a corner of the ceiling. 'Still got that damp patch. Up there, where it's beginning to peel. I remember it from that last time I nicked you.'

'You should nick some of them blokes from the council,' blazed Shena.

Terry Jackson, still not looking at Roach, said: 'I'm clean, Ted.'

From behind him Lines said: 'Then you've got nothing to worry about, have you?'

Shena put an arm out in a worried, protective gesture towards her daughter, who leaned against her and solemnly watched the two detectives.

Roach held out a piece of paper. It was not the scrap

acquired by Young and Loxton, but a small sheet of typing paper on which the car number had been typed. 'That your registration number? And would the vehicle be a sort of rusty blue?'

'Yeah, sure. I got papers. Bought it down the road.'

'I know.'

They heard the front door open noisily. 'That'll be Sally,' said Shena Jackson, thankful for the opportunity of taking the eight-year-old out of the room to her older sister. After she had gone and closed the door behind her, Roach let the silence draw out for as long as it could be stretched. At last he said:

'Has anyone borrowed that car recently? It was seen this morning, early hours. At a building site. The driver dumped some rubbish.'

Jackson shrugged. 'So I dumped a few things.'

'What things?'

'Garden stuff.' As Lines and Roach exchanged a glance, Jackson began to push himself upright on the sofa. 'The council dump was closed. It's not a crime, is it?'

'Unauthorized dumping. Mm. Quite a few byelaws against that kind of thing.'

'Look, I'm going straight, Ted. I've got the kids to think about.'

'What were you dumping?'

'I've told you, garden rubbish.'

'And what else?'

'Oh, for God's sake.'

'If you can't tell us here,' said Roach, getting to his feet, 'you'd better come down the station and tell us there. Tell us the lot.'

Lines stood above him. Reluctantly Jackson heaved himself up out of the sofa. His expression was one that Roach wearily recognized from long, long experience. He had seen it so often before, on so many different faces. Only at a time like this the faces weren't different but predictably the same: not so much resignation as built-in enmity, a determination not to co-operate even if co-operation would do no harm. If Jackson was really going straight, his automatic attitude was still one of stubborn hostility.

In the kitchen doorway, Shena Jackson was frozen into fear. The two girls, one taller than the other but still shy and uncertain, peeped out from behind her.

'All right, girls. We're just borrowing your Dad.'

Jackson set up a grumble. 'I've got to sign on this morning.'

'Ted,' protested Shena. 'He was here all night.'

'Who said anything about last night?'

Jackson lapsed into silence as he got into the car. He was still silent, his head sullenly down, as they crossed Sun Hill yard towards the custody area.

Roach stopped outside the door. He could sense that Jackson was growing increasingly nervous. Perhaps this was the time to strike and get it all wrapped up without too much time wasted indoors. 'I've always played you fair, Terry. So let's get it over with. Keep it simple. Put your hands up and I'll tone it all down, tell the brief to go easy. You know me.'

'I'm clean, Ted.'

'Terry, Terry . . . all right, I know you tried, but like I said, old habits . . .'

'Ask Shena.'

'Now come on, Terry. You've known me long enough.'

'Ted.' Tosh Lines broke the flow. 'Shouldn't we book him in?'

Roach glared, but pushed the door open and led the way in. Since Tosh had been so eager to go through the motions, Tosh could get on with handling the routine. Roach went on towards the Computer Aided Despatch room to see if anything of interest had cropped up while they had been out.

He was presented with an unexpected bonus. Norika Datta saw his hazy reflection in her VDU screen and turned with a sheet of notes torn off her pad. They fitted beautifully into the pattern. A burglary had been reported from last night. June Ackland and Reg Hollis were already on the scene, and there was a witness. A VCR and CD player had been stolen; and the serial numbers matched the articles recovered from the building site.

Ted Roach smiled.

Two minutes later he was not smiling.

'He's done *what*?'

'It was bound to happen,' said Sergeant Bob Cryer dismally. 'But did it have to happen on Barton Street's patch?'

Word had just leaked through that, as Cryer had put it, the inevitable had at last happened. On his way home from a pub, Sergeant Tom Penny had been picked up and breathalysed. They had known – none better than Bob Cryer – that Penny had given up even a pretence of the social drink or two with his colleagues in the *Freemason's Arms*, and guessed that he was in the habit of slinking off somewhere else. Now they had discovered where that somewhere else was.

'You'd think he had a death wish,' groaned Roach. 'To pick one that close to enemy territory . . . !'

Barton Street police station had never been on friendly terms with Sun Hill; least of all since the period when they had shared premises during the Sun Hill rebuilding. It was Tom Penny who had accused one of their sergeants of using a Sun Hill prisoner as a punchbag, and refused to back down in spite of moves to smooth it all over. The fact that the accusation had been true, and that the sergeant was later found to be a crook anyway, did not endear Penny to the Barton Street team.

Now they had their opportunity for revenge, and it was their turn not to back down.

Penny had been picked up on the grounds that his car had a faulty brake light. Breathalysed, he had been only just over the odds; but it was enough. No doubt he had tried to argue with the custody sergeant at Barton Street, but with all those memories piled up behind him, there was little chance of any operation of the old pals' act.

'Don't tell me he wasn't set up,' growled Ted Roach. 'I bet that once they'd found his regular boozer, they were waiting every night for a chance.'

'I'm not taking that bet,' said Cryer. 'But it's still his own stupid bloody fault. Set-up or not, he was over the limit and he had to be charged, police sergeant or not.'

'And now what? Any hope of intervention from on high?' He thought of the Chief Superintendent, and said: 'What's Brownlow going to say about it?'

Cryer shuddered. 'I can just imagine. I'll be off duty when he gets back, thank God.'

'Back?'

'On that two-day course. Special techniques for the higher-ups. Along with your beloved Alastair.'

'Oh, yes. Golden boy Greig.'

Ted Roach had forgotten that his fellow detective sergeant was being allowed time off to attend a very senior two-day course at training college. Alastair Greig knew how to make just the right noises and ensure that they were heard by just the right people. Roach assured himself that he wasn't resentful: senior he might be, but he wouldn't have enjoyed that sort of thing anyway, wasting time in a classroom when there was so much waiting to be done out of doors. In that, at least, he and DI Burnside saw eye to eye.

'It'll be Conway's job, anyway,' he pointed out, 'to break it to the Chief Super.'

'And Conway happens to be on that same whizzkids' freebie.'

'Who the hell's minding the shop, then?'

'I'm not just here as an ornament,' said Cryer. 'But we've got Inspector Monroe on the premises, of course. And strictly speaking it'll be Monroe's job to break the news to Conway.'

'Which brings it down to who's going to break it to Monroe. That's not a pretty thought, either.'

They did not dare to ask what the chances were of a swift intervention with Barton Street to try and hush the whole thing up. Or what would happen to Tom Penny when Barton Street self-righteously rejected any kind of cover-up and went ahead with a prosecution.

Ted Roach thought of the number of times he might have been picked up in similar condition; and shivered.

Chief Inspector Derek Conway was indeed on the two-day course, and not enjoying it. At the end of the first day he had spent the evening, like the rest of them, trundling out an essay on everything he knew about Public Relations and the prescribed theme of 'Police Image in the Modern Society', and in the morning had been awarded a C-minus. So much for hands-on policing and the fruits of years of experience.

He supposed he would have to go into the bar and face them before lunch, and hoped there would not be too many questions asked about everybody's relative grades.

In the general buzz of conversation close to the bar he could hear the familiar timbre of Chief Superintendent Brownlow holding forth. That voice gave the impression of being well satisfied with results so far. It was noticeable, thought Conway sourly, that although there were plenty of Supers and Chief Supers milling around, Brownlow had felt more at home pontificating to a mere detective sergeant.

'It's a lesson we need to get right through,' he was saying to Alastair Greig. 'Distance and division among the ranks only divides us from the public we're trying to serve.' He flapped his conference file, with his essay clipped uppermost. 'As well as covering the general field I think I've managed to introduce the aspects most relevant to our own local circumstances. I'll run you off a copy.'

'Thank you, sir.'

Brownlow had not seen Conway edge into the room. A few comradely laughs from the other top brass near the bar finally tugged at his attention, and he sauntered off to join them. The volume of his voice was not reduced. 'I was just saying I ought to pass yesterday's essay on to the men. Not bad, Bplus, mm? Of course it's an area I've studied.' He nodded towards Greig, now standing alone on a far stretch of carpet. 'That's why I recommended our most promising young CID man for this session. Do him good, being here, meeting people.'

Greig was all too obviously not meeting a soul. Conway, hesitating between the senior officers it might be politic to make up to, and Greig, turned coward and chose Greig.

'Hello, guv.'

'Oh, don't guv me, Alastair. Not here. You'll get a sore throat guvving this little lot.' As Conway heard Brownlow's voice raised again in pontifical mood, he asked casually: 'And how did your own essay go?'

'I got an A,' said Greig quietly, looking at Brownlow across the room.

Conway was tempted to tell him to wipe that complacent smile off his face. Greig still had the basic conviction that when it came down to it you could make it on this job by scoring good marks and waiting to be promoted on sheer theoretical merit. He was cunning at insinuating himself into his superiors' good graces, but still hadn't quite got his priorities right. It would take him time to balance out the essentials. Alastair Greig was never going to make the Catholic Guild, he wasn't in the Lodge, so where did he go from here? If he had any sense he would buy the college tie, tell everyone he had been here on this prestigious course and never mind the marks: get drunk with these clowns after the waffle, and next time they were drunk they might remember him and recommend a promotion. But you didn't talk to pushy young sergeants like that. Let them find out for themselves.

They all had a quick, not madly-appetizing lunch, and trooped back to the seminar room. Conway sat awkwardly on a hard chair and noticed that in this atmosphere, at any rate, Greig looked quite at home. The very way he sat betokened eager interest and commitment to whatever was going on.

So he had been awarded a Grade A, on a subject which he had never properly encountered in real life and on which he was likely to find the theories didn't apply when you really got down to the nitty-gritty.

They sat in a semi-circle while Crampton, the course leader, placed himself beside his whiteboard. Behind him, tantalizingly, was a detailed model of a cluster of town streets with blocks of flats and a cluster of shops. Any kid would have been happy to play with it for hours. But Conway had an idea that it was not here just to be played with. Sooner or later they would find out something about it. Maybe some earnest attention was called for. Crampton, a genial man in his fifties, was not a policeman but an academic, and Conway still felt tetchily that he was an ivory tower philosopher, not used to being down on the ground where theory met bloody-minded violence head on. At the same time there was a disturbing curl to Crampton's lips which suggested that he knew many of them here were just humouring him, and that he had got the measure of them all.

'Now, on this whole subject of the principles of policing,' he said amiably, 'your essays came up with a number of interesting suggestions. Some were, if I may say so, rather familiar generalizations. Others struck out in fresh directions. Mr Brownlow, particularly, offered some helpful pointers.' Even while Brownlow's modest smile was still puckering his lips, Crampton was going on: 'But only one of you pointed out that image and reality never resemble each other.' He was careful not to name names this time, but his glance at Greig was indicative enough. Brownlow's smile faded. 'So let's dismiss all this nonsense about appearances and what people think about us or ought to be persuaded to think about us. Let's take a long, honest look at what we really are.'

He moved the whiteboard to one side and invited them to form small groups around the perimeter of the model. Each

99

group was provided with a sketch map, some more detailed diagrams, and pads of plain drawing paper. The basic story was of a siege. A gunman had killed one man, and holed himself up on the fourth floor of a block of flats with three hostages, two of them women. Ground rules had been laid down about the number of cars available, and the limited TSG back-up because of the prior needs of a demo that was getting out of hand on the far side of the city. After allowing fifteen minutes for discussion, pointing out that this was far less than they might be offered in a real emergency, Crampton began moving from one group to another to see what plans they had devised.

Brownlow, Conway and Greig stood at one corner of the board studying a back alley and a row of lock-up garages, beautifully modelled to scale.

'How's the gunman?' Crampton challenged them. 'Is he ready to break?'

Conway stared down a very convincing street. It was almost possible to visualize a tiny figure racing down the stairwell and out at an angle across the patch of trodden earth at the bottom, across the street and into a network of side streets. He left it to Brownlow to outline their tactics.

'We've sealed off the area, blocks here' – Brownlow's finger jabbed at one end of the back alley and one street corner – 'and here. Sergeants in these positions. And an inspector to liaise with the Press.'

'Ah, yes. The Press. And where are they?'

Brownlow indicated a cul-de-sac behind the row of local shops. 'Here, out of harm's way.'

'But they'll want to be out where they can take pictures.'

'We'll explain the problem.'

'They'll sneak round you.'

'In which case,' Conway interposed, 'I'd arrest them.'

'For what?'

'Obstruction.'

Crampton leaned over the block of flats in the centre of the model. 'So your gunman's up here, mouthing obscenities from the window and getting his hostages more and more terrified, and you're wrangling with the Press?'

'Marksmen, sir,' said Brownlow curtly. 'On these roofs. And down here, behind cover.'

'To shoot reporters?'

Brownlow tried to keep patient and authoritative. He turned towards the whiteboard on which he had drawn a pyramid. At the top was 'CH. SUP.', and below it various sections defining specific areas of responsibility in the situation.

Conway was aware of Crampton repressing a tolerant little smile, and guessed that something quietly lethal was coming.

'And where precisely are you, Mr Brownlow?'

'At the top here. Supervising and co-ordinating. I've alerted – '

'And you?' Crampton interrupted him and swung suddenly towards Conway. 'What are you up to?'

'I'm in charge of the forces on the street, personally conducting– '

'And you?' Crampton snapped at Greig.

'I'm talking to the gunman.'

'So who's controlling all this?'

'I suppose,' said Conway, 'it's Superintendent Brownlow.'

'Not at all. It's this fellow.' Crampton jerked his head at Greig. 'Your pyramid is upside-down, Mr Brownlow.' He wiped the figure off the board and drew another one, inverted. 'Now, this is where the action's happening. And this man, your detective sergeant, is the key. Every word he says, every thought he thinks, can make or break the whole operation. Your main job is only to support that.' Again he was looking at Greig. 'So what are you responding to?'

'The gunman?'

'So,' asked Crampton again, 'who is controlling all this?'

'It certainly isn't the criminal,' said Brownlow. 'Or shouldn't be.'

'Worrying, isn't it?'

Crampton moved on to the next group.

Brownlow stared for a moment at the model and then at the whiteboard. It was clear to Conway's sceptical eye that the Chief Super was already assembling reasons for exculpating himself from any errors of judgement – or, as he was probably already describing it, errors of interpretation by others. In Brownlow's mind the pyramid was already resettling itself right way up.

He said busily: 'Something I must check with Andrew. I'll leave you to think this exercise over while I go and phone.'

When he had gone, Conway said: 'Well, what d'you know? All these years we've been standing on our heads.' He could only hope that there wasn't an actual siege and a possible shoot-out going on for real while their backs were turned. Interesting to see what course of action Brownlow would take if something really had cropped up.

June Ackland and Reg Hollis were on the scene, as notified to Ted Roach, but at first had seemed to make little progress. Outside the door of the two-storey council maisonette was a cluster of full milk bottles, and two local free papers were stuffed into the letterbox. It was always a worrying sight. The milk ought to have been in by now if it had not, on this estate, already been nicked.

Mrs Cox, the elderly neighbour who had called them, was shaking her head, waiting to see some results.

'Maybe they're having a lie-in,' suggested Ackland.

'Shouldn't think so. It's bright and early in there most days.'

'Did you hear anything unusual last night?'

'I might have.'

'Like what?' asked Reg Hollis, trying to look keen, though this did not come naturally to him.

'Well . . . screams.'

Ackland looked at Hollis. He tried to look not just keen but masterful, and drove his shoulder against the door. At the third attempt it gave way. No doubt Hollis would be putting

102

in for sick leave and specialist treatment for an injured shoulder after this.

The door led straight into a sitting-room. Like so many others on this estate it might have been untidy as a general rule, but surely never like this. Pictures had been wrenched from the walls. A table was turned over, and papers were scattered wildly across the floor. A pile of CDs and LPs stood heaped unevenly beside an empty space by one wall. From a television set dangled leads which must once have been connected to a VCR.

There was no sound.

Apprehensively Reg Hollis made for the open plan staircase to the upper floor. June Ackland paused for a moment, digging a CD operator's manual from the debris and checking the serial number and description. Then Hollis was calling for her; and she didn't like the note of anxiety in his voice.

She followed him upstairs. Hollis was standing in the bedroom doorway, looking in. She moved past him. The room looked as untidy as the one downstairs, with a bedside lamp halfway across the floor, the corners of the carpet rumpled up, and the contents of a dressing-table drawer tossed all over the place. The bed against the wall was a large one, heaped with a tangle of bedclothes. There was nobody in it; but on the floor, huddled into a corner, was a young woman, motionless, silent . . . but not dead.

She wore a blue nightdress which had been ripped from one shoulder. There was blood on the hem of the dress and down one leg, sprawled out in front of her. When she looked up, slowly and blankly, there were bruises down the left side of her face.

Ackland spoke very slowly and gently. 'Hello. My name's June. Can I come in? We're from the police.'

The face remained blank.

'It's all right now, love.' Ackland made a move to help the girl up, but she wriggled backwards as if to tuck herself even more securely against the wall. 'What's your name?'

103

There was no reply.

Hollis, finishing a brisk call on his radio, said: 'Do you live here?'

She shook her head.

'Look,' said Hollis, 'we'd like to find out who did this to you.'

Ackland felt a prickle of alarm. The girl was coming slowly back to reality, but was already frightened by it: terribly frightened by something. 'Reg . . .'

'He's out there now, somewhere,' Hollis blundered on. 'And we stand a good chance of getting him if you – '

The girl howled once, let it die away, and slumped forward with her head on her knees.

'A doctor,' said June Ackland. 'And quickly. And we'll have to get her somewhere more comfortable. Somewhere she can feel safe.'

Eight

Brownlow returned from his telephone call late, settling into the semi-circle with a grim face and trying to concentrate on what the course leader was saying. Conway saw that it was taking a great effort; and that the concentration was never more than intermittent.

'We're there,' Crampton continued, gesturing towards the model of the siege, 'because we believe that what that man has committed is a crime. Beliefs and opinions are what drive our actions, but most of the time we hardly consider them. What's really in our mind to back it all up? What *is* the Police?' He looked directly at Greig. 'You out there on your megaphone, what are you thinking about?'

'I'm worried about the hostages.'

'Commendable. Of course, though, that will show in your voice.'

'I'd try not to show it.'

'Good. It's a busy area, though, isn't it? You're anxious not to show your feelings. Not just anxious. You're dead worried. In this situation, is that going to be helpful? Or not?'

'I suppose it's not.' said Greig.

'So what else?' He turned towards Brownlow. 'What's it like from your angle?'

'I want to make sure the whole operation works out right. The whole thing.'

'Why?'

Brownlow looked fazed for a moment, then shook himself into life. He said, slightly patronizingly: 'Well, that's my job.'

'So you'd better get it right or you'll lose your job?'

105

Brownlow took alarm. 'I didn't say that.'

'You didn't have to. But we all feel it, don't we? Sergeant, I'll bet you're thinking, "Get this right and I'll make DI." Wouldn't it cross your mind?'

'Yes,' said Greig frankly.

'That's all a great weight. All the considerations, prejudices, weighing it down, slowing it all down. Hence reactive policing. You know the terms: proactive is timely and right, reactive is too late. And isn't most policing reactive? And why? Because instead of hitting the critical nub of action we're either fast asleep or dithering about our image.' Crampton perched himself casually on the edge of the table, turning his back on the whiteboard and the model. 'You must have asked yourselves the question: what the hell am I doing here? In the absence of answers we plod on like robots. So just what are we doing here, gentlemen? What are we *for*?'

'Upholding the law,' said one superintendent who looked as disdainful at such footling questions as Conway felt.

'What about the gunman's law? The law of his own liberty and self-preservation. That's a law, too.'

'It isn't the right law, though.'

'Can we say that?'

'It isn't the law of the land,' another pupil contributed.

'Neither was the French Resistance. Our gunman might be thinking you're just a bunch of bullies about to prevail simply because you've got the clout.'

'That's his opinion.'

'So what's yours?'

Greig said: 'That he's wrong.'

'That's your opinion. You'll win because you've got the firepower, but that doesn't make one opinion better than any other.'

There was a buzz of resentment. 'The maniac's killed somebody . . .'

'So do soldiers.'

'He's killed somebody innocent.'

106

'So do soldiers. *C'est la guerre.*'

'I'd like to know where this is getting us,' complained a superintendent. 'I came here to learn something about policing, upholding the law . . .'

Greig said 'Sir.' There was something in his complacent tone that convinced Conway he was about to come out with another bit of mark-scoring sanctimoniousness.

'Yes?'

'You said this is just our opinion, but . . . this may sound a bit simple, but . . . I *know* he's wrong. That's all. Killing innocent people in these circumstances, for selfish ends, *is* wrong. No benefit of the doubt. I can't say why, but it's . . . it's why I'm a policeman.'

Crampton nodded approval. 'Welcome to the real world.'

At the end of the session, Conway noticed Greig hanging back to talk to Crampton, presumably in the hope of consolidating his gains. He didn't seem to mind who else heard, either.

'What's my own view?' Crampton was answering Greig's respectful question. 'Oh, I'm just a gadfly, engaged to shake up your brains a bit. It's up to you yourself to think about why you joined. You must have respected the concept of abstract law if you chose to serve it with your life.'

'It's a good career.'

'Oh, that comes later. Look, if we don't ask, it's just a crude set-up of them and us, ignorance and habit feeding each other. Your criminal knows it. But he's locked in stupidity. Part of your job is to remind him who he is, and you might find he'll be grateful to you.' He looked past Greig and smiled. 'Making sense to you, Mr Conway?'

'If anything in this job made sense to me, sir, I'd write a book and retire. Or maybe retire and *then* write the book. Safer that way.' In the corridor he caught up with Brownlow. 'Everything all right back in the nick, sir?'

'No, Derek, it's not all right. I really think I'll have to skip the closing session and get back.'

A useful get-out, whatever it is, thought Conway cynically; but kept the thought to himself. 'That bad? Maybe I'm the one who ought to – '

'You stay here, Derek, and concentrate on the course. I'll concentrate on Penny before it's too late.'

'Penny? What the devil's Penny been up to?'

Brownlow told him. And Conway, sickeningly, knew in his bones that it was already too late.

Ted Roach reached the maisonette in good humour. Even the sight of the devastated sitting-room did not depress him. It was just going to make things worse for Terry Jackson. This time they could really throw the book at him. He had already confessed to the unlawful dumping of garden waste on private property, hoping that that would be the end of it. But there was going to be a hell of a lot more than that before Roach had finished.

If anything could have damped his good spirits, it was June Ackland's face. She was a good officer, a tough girl, and not one to give way easily. But her face looked downright tragic; and she was far from respectful about his theories.

'Terry Jackson? He's a treacle and brown paper boy. But all this . . .' She invited him to study the chaos all around them.

'Attila the bloody Hun,' he conceded.

'And Terry's a family man, isn't he?'

'So was Attila. Right,' said Roach briskly, 'where's this witness?'

Ackland was staring at him with dread, as if she didn't want him to take another step. She might almost have been a suspect, scared of his next move, scared stiff for her own safety. Only June Ackland was rarely scared for her own safety.

A man came downstairs and into the room. Roach had dealt with Dr Wyndham before, and nodded a welcome. He liked to know who he was dealing with.

Wyndham was holding a pair of tights and a dressing-gown

108

cord. 'Her hands had been tied and her mouth gagged. She'd obviously got free before you lot arrived. We'll have to tread lightly on this. She won't be easy to move.'

This was not quite what Roach had anticipated. He had come expecting the promised witness. There had been no talk about anyone being tied up and maltreated. Ackland had been right: this was not Terry Jackson country, at all. 'Has she been injured?'

'I won't know until I've examined her properly. Right now she's in shock, which is serious enough. There's some blood, probably from a graze on her wrist where she was tied.'

'Have you asked her?'

'Yes, I've asked her. She's very disturbed, sergeant.'

'Mind if I try?'

'Yes,' said Wyndham fiercely, 'I do mind.'

'I suppose I can live with that.' Roach headed for the stairs.

'Sarge,' Ackland appealed, 'she's not up to it.'

'I've got a suspect locked up. If he didn't do it, somebody else did, and I need to know. I'll go easy, June, don't you worry.'

Wyndham said indignantly: 'You're contravening unequivocal medical advice.'

'I'll bear that in mind.'

Roach reached the top of the stairs, slowed, and knew Ackland was following him up. He did not wait for her to reach the landing before going on into the bedroom.

It came as another shock to see the girl slumped on the edge of the bed. This had not been at all the picture he had built up in his own mind. A clumsy robbery, yes; and a clumsy attempt to ditch the stuff – though they still hadn't figured out why Jackson had been in such a hurry to get rid of something he had only just lifted. But this stunned, blank-eyed victim was way out of that league.

He needed answers; and needed them fast, before they all went off down a wrong trail.

'Can I come in?' He kept his voice hushed. When there was

109

no reply, he advanced a few cautious steps, set an overturned chair back on its legs, and sat down. Ackland was in the doorway, watching him accusingly. 'I'm a policeman,' he said. 'We don't have much respect for privacy, either. The name's Ted. Detective Sergeant Ted Roach from Sun Hill CID.' He waited, but she had given him only one frightened glance and now was looking into space, past his left shoulder. 'I've seen a few things in my time. This sort of thing, too. Doesn't make it any easier, but you can talk to me if you want to.'

Ackland shifted a foot warningly. The girl made not the slightest movement.

'You see,' said Roach earnestly, 'I want to find out who did this. That's my job.' He leaned forward. 'Are you hurt?' No answer. This promised to be hard going. 'Did you see who did this? Okay' – he made it brighter, a bit pushier – 'there's a few things I can work out for myself. Someone broke in, right? Were you upstairs? Here, upstairs?' He gave her a few more seconds, then said: 'Look, you don't have to speak to me, but I've told you my name. What about yours?'

At last there was a response. It came as little more than a whisper. 'Jennifer.'

'Mine's really Edward in full, but calling me that's an arrest-able offence where I work. So . . . Jenny?'

She nodded.

'Sarge,' said Ackland.

He was not going to let himself be interrupted now, just when he was making a breakthrough. He turned threaten-ingly towards her. 'If you want to nurse a victim, Ackland, go and nurse Hollis.'

She went.

He turned back to Jenny. 'We've made a start. But let's take it gently. Do you know why I'm asking these questions? Because I'm a policeman, and policemen can't help but ask stupid questions when it's the last thing anybody wants. Any time you want me to stop, just say so or shake your head, make a noise, anything. I'm not famous for my sensitivity.'

He paused. 'Let's try an easy question, anyway: do you live here?'

She shook her head. But she was looking at him now, plaintive and unsure, yet somehow interested in what he might say next. It was like drawing somebody very carefully and delicately out of a quicksand, not letting go but not forcing the pace too dangerously. She was still unsure of talking, but she was ready to nod or shake her head. He established that she was looking after the place for a friend: a girlfriend, not a boyfriend. She had had a boyfriend, but not any more. No, they couldn't contact him. No, she hadn't been here long. Only a few days.

Now came the awkward bit. She seemed to trust him now, but he knew how easily fright could turn things round again. He couldn't put things right for her, or make up for what she'd gone through while the thief ransacked the place, but he was damn well going to lumber somebody with the responsibility for it.

He tried a serious, reassuring smile. 'What exactly happened last night?'

She uttered not so much a cry as a despairing, long-drawn-out whimper.

'I'll stop if you want me to,' said Roach.

'But you won't. I know you won't.'

Before he could say any more, Hollis put his head round the door. 'Sarge, the ambulance.'

'Two minutes,' growled Roach. When Hollis had slunk away, he said: 'We're going to get you to the hospital.'

'What for?'

'They can see if you're hurt.' When she shook her head as if to deny any of this, to keep her distance and not be touched, he said: 'But of course you're hurt. Where does the blood come from?'

'I was . . . he tied . . .'

'Okay.' Time was running out. 'Can you tell me from the beginning? You were here – up here?'

'Yes'

'Asleep?'

Slowly, in a hideously clinging dream, Jenny fumbled to tell her story. She chanted it in an undertone rather than speaking it, and occasionally stopped to shake her head as if to deny everything she had just said. It was all too simple and predictable; but not simple for the one who had undergone it.

She had been half asleep when she heard something downstairs and went down to see what it was. A man was standing in a corner of the sitting-room, stooping to tug a plug from the wall. She screamed. She had not wanted to, but she just couldn't help it. And once started, she couldn't stop screaming. The man grabbed her and begged her to stop. 'But I couldn't, I just couldn't stop.' Roach could imagine it all too well. The intruder was getting frightened, might well have backed off and made a getaway without any more trouble if only she would stop yelling. He had probably been watching the place for some time, knew the owner was away, had not been expecting anyone on the premises. He could have been as scared as she was when she appeared on the scene. But he didn't run. He grabbed her, struggled with her. She fell, grabbed at things, started throwing things at him, while he kept begging her to shut up. Then she made a dash for the stairs and got up to the bedroom and tried to close the door. Only he kept coming, pushing his way in.

He told her he was only after things, she needn't be frightened. Insured things – she wouldn't lose any money, and he was the one who really needed it. When she went on howling and grabbing for things to throw at him, he got a hold on her and started tying her hands and shoving some sort of gag into her mouth.

Jenny stared back into the past, only half believing what had happened to her. 'I couldn't do anything. And then he started . . . he stroked my face . . .'

Ackland had come in, more determined than Hollis. 'Sarge. The ambulance.'

Roach got up, nodding. As they watched the girl being lifted into the ambulance, he said: 'You'd better go with her.'

June Ackland looked at him, surprised, almost grateful.

Bob Cryer drew up outside Tom Penny's house. He was in civvies and in his own car. He sat in it for a full minute while the radio pumped out some mindless pop which he would normally never have had on. He found it hard to summon up the will to switch it off and get out of the car. When at last he managed it, he walked very slowly up the path to the front door, and again hesitated for what seemed an eternity before ringing the bell.

Wendy Penny's expression was full of foreboding as she opened the door, but changed to one of relief as she saw who it was. As she stood back to let him in, he put a hand lightly on her arm.

'Can you cope with this?'

'Who else is going to?'

The lounge of Sergeant Tom Penny's home was tidy enough, clean and bright enough, yet somehow lifeless. It felt as if nothing ever really happened in here, though at the moment Tom was sitting at a writing desk, its pigeonholes stuffed with what might be household bills and unanswered letters. He was staring at the wall above it as if seeking inspiration for something to add to the scribbled lines on a pad open in front of him. He did not look best pleased to be interrupted, but slowly put down his pen and closed the pad when Bob Cryer was shown in.

Cryer said: 'Those slags at Barton Street have shafted you good and proper. Sorry, mate.'

It might have been the first time someone had put it the way Tom Penny himself saw it. He managed a wry smile. 'You want a beer? Don't worry' – he intercepted a quick glance from his wife to Cryer – 'I'm not going to get legless and do a technicolour yawn over Conway or Brownlow when I get there.'

'Just the one, then.'

Wendy brought them two cans of beer, her face strained as she handed over supplies of the stuff that had already done so much damage. When she had gone, the place felt even more cold and unlived-in. But Tom Penny was going to have to get used to the idea of spending a lot of his time here from now on. Remembering past troubles between Tom and Wendy, Bob Cryer wondered how they would adjust.

He said: 'You realize Monroe'll be waiting for you when you go in tonight? And then there'll be Brownlow. Take a word of advice, and don't – '

'I wasn't pissed, Bob. Nowhere near.'

'I'm sure you weren't,' said Cryer soothingly.

'I was as safe as ninety per cent of the people on the road.'

'Sure.'

'I'm not taking it lying down,' Penny raged. 'I'll tell you that right here and now.'

'I don't see . . . I mean, just what d'you think you can do?'

'I know the form all right. What they'll be expecting of me. In and out of court in double-quick time, plea of guilty, fine and disqualification, resign on medical grounds. Keep the dirt under the carpet.'

'You're saying there's an alternative?'

'I know I'll end up kicked into the gutter. But you can go out fighting.'

'How? Do a floor-show in court? Come on, Tom. What's the point? How can you plead not guilty?'

Penny gulped fiercely at his beer. 'How can the slags we deal with all day plead not guilty?'

'Driving over the limit isn't like other crimes,' Cryer pointed out. 'It's not about the state of your mind, what your intentions were. There's no room for blowing smoke. In driving over the limit, guilt is a fact of biochemistry.'

'You're just like the others. You want me to curl up and die. Nice and quietly, so it doesn't disturb the rest of you.'

114

'No, I want you to stop looking up your own orifice and deal with the real world.'

'You mean I go crawling after a medical discharge, along with all the old toe-rags who've been copped taking back-handers?'

Cryer might have guessed that Tom Penny's attitude would be one of defiance and accusation. It had been like that all too often in Sun Hill: always somebody else's fault, a persecution complex, an inability to keep his voice down or his temper down.

'Not like them,' he said patiently. 'You're entitled to a full medical discharge and no reservations. You've not been a fully fit man since that shooting – '

'That's right, throw that in my face. Tom Penny wasn't up to the job.'

Sadly it was true. Maybe not Penny's fault entirely, but true. Largely the fault of the man who had shot him in that business eighteen months ago. Penny had never really got over it. He was not up to the job, and that was that. If he had gone on much longer he would have been elbowed out even if he hadn't got nicked. Everyone in Sun Hill knew it, apart from Penny himself.

If he stubbornly refused to resign on medical grounds and forced them to sack him, what would his references look like when he went in search of other employment? With decent references he could walk into a security firm tomorrow – one of the respectable ones, with plenty of ex-job people to work along with.

'Look,' Cryer said, 'the way things are, you've got twenty-five years in, right? You resign as a sergeant and you're qualified for your full pension when that's due, and a tidy lump sum now. If you drive them to sack you, they don't have to give you your full pension.'

'Anything to keep the skeletons safe in the cupboard: that's what it comes down to.'

'Be realistic, Tom.'

'God Almighty, Bob, where's the justice?'

'Justice?' Cryer could not repress a smile. 'Aren't you a bit old to believe in Father Christmas?'

At last Tom Penny, too, managed to force a sickly, reluctant smile. It disappeared when he glanced at the clock on the mantelpiece and said: 'I suppose I'd better be getting ready. Go in and face them.'

'Yes. I think you'd better. And Tom . . . play it gently. For your own sake.'

June Ackland and Reg Hollis sat in the cramped reception area of the casualty department. Hollis was far from being Ackland's idea of a soul-mate. Even as a fellow officer on routine duties he could usually be a pain in several parts of the anatomy. But waiting, sipping coffee from plastic cups, for once they were glad of each other's company.

A doctor pushed his way through swing doors and marched past. Hollis jumped up and tried to intercept him, but was ignored. Another pair of doors swung to, and the man was gone. Hollis made another stab, this time at a passing nurse. She shook her head. 'You'll have to speak to the doctor.'

So much for the respect accorded a police uniform.

Ackland rubbed her tired eyes and said: 'Do you know Terry Jackson?'

'You hum it, I'll play it.'

She was in no mood for that sort of cheap jibe. 'He wouldn't have done that,' she insisted. 'He's a petty thief. He burgles empty houses and takes a few things. He doesn't wreck the place, he doesn't beat people up.'

'Maybe he didn't.'

'I wish we knew.'

The doctor came striding importantly back, but this time condescended to slow and come to a halt in front of the two officers.

'You brought Miss Whittaker in?'

'How is she?'

'We've patched up the cuts – well, grazes, nothing more than that. No specific injuries. She's very brave, but she'll need somebody with her for a while.'

June Ackland breathed a sigh of relief. 'Not too awful, then.'

'We've taken swabs, of course. You'll be getting the pathology report just as soon as possible.'

'Swabs?'

The doctor looked at her curiously. 'That's customary in cases of alleged rape, isn't it?'

Nine

The interview room reeked of Ted Roach's crushed cigarette butts. No suspect had yet thought of registering an official complaint about the torture of passive smoking, but when the day came it might throw one of Roach's investigations right off the rails. He stabbed another fag into the ashtray, and waited for Tosh Lines to escort their current suspect in. Just for once DS Roach was unsure of what he wanted to come out of this. He couldn't believe what all the evidence told him. Which did not mean that he was going to let Jackson off lightly.

The formalities were gone through. The tape recorder was set turning, and it was announced that an interview was taking place between Detective Sergeant Roach and Terence Andrew Jackson, with Detective Constable Lines in attendance. Jackson's rights had been duly advised. And Jackson, Roach was happy to see, was sweating.

Only it still didn't make sense. Not violence, not with bumbling Terry. You couldn't even call him a light-fingered crook. Everything he did was crude and heavy.

Only not getting rough with girls.

Roach said: 'Right. Here we are again. Now for starters, how's the money situation, Terry? Coping?'

'Just about.'

'Expensive little jacket Sally had on.'

'Oxfam shop.'

Roach knew a lie when he heard one, and was content to let its echoes fizz around the interview room. He contemplated the suspect, and remembered the last time. Terry Jackson had worn just the same hangdog look, and been just as glib with pathetic excuses; and had got two years, but served only nine months. This time . . . well, it all depended.

Jackson was unhappy with the long silence. He blurted out: 'Look, Ted, you know I've gone clean. All right, so I shouldn't have dumped stuff on a building site.'

'What stuff?'

'I told you. Garden rubbish. Rose clippings, bits of an old chair.'

'Terry, you know I wouldn't have you in here for dumping rubbish. You know that.'

'What I don't know is what I'm in here for.'

Roach kept him waiting a moment or two, then said: 'We found a CD player, VCR, cash, a silk scarf, and a food mixer. Just your kind of stuff.'

'Anybody's.'

'Garden rubbish, you'd call it? Must have some powerful fertilizer. Care to tell me the brand? And why,' asked Roach with sudden venom, 'did you dump it? Why not sell it like you've been selling hot gear for years? What made you lose your bottle and chuck your winnings away, Terry? Come on. We've had our laughs together, good and bad times, but look at me very carefully. Look at me straight, Terry. Am I laughing now?'

He knew what he was after. It had to start with Terry Jackson, but there was no way he was going to believe it ended there. Let Jackson admit to creeping in the way he always did, not making a sound, finding an open door and collecting the gear and getting out without trouble. Get Jackson out of the way and then work out what could have happened after he had gone.

'I don't know what you're on about,' Jackson mumbled.

'You did the job,' said Roach. 'Only a burglary. Get that out of the way, and the rest might make sense.'

He was offering Jackson a get-out, and it looked as if it was going to be accepted.

Jackson licked his lips. 'That's all you'd do me for?'

'Come on. Was that a yes?'

'I don't know.'

There was something wrong, something wildly askew somewhere. For the first time, looking at the hangdog, sweating Jackson, he wondered if the straightforward categorization was dead wrong. Terry Jackson wasn't just going through the motions. He was scared stiff, and there was something seriously wrong.

Roach got to his feet and leaned over Jackson. 'Let's have it straight. Why did you dump the stuff?'

The door of the interview room opened to admit DCI Wray. His perpetually mistrustful eyes took in the scene, and his scratchy voice said: 'Can I have a word with you, Ted?'

The recorder was switched off, and Tosh Lines escorted Terry Jackson back to his cell for lunch.

Outside the interview room, watching them go, Wray said: 'What was that supposed to be?'

Ted Roach, furious at being interrupted just when he had been sure of moving in really effectively on Jackson, said: 'Guv, he was ready to break.'

'Or be broken. About to get thumped, the way I saw it.'

Roach could not be bothered to deny it. Sod Wray, sod the lot of them, busting in or getting legalistic just when there was a chance of getting a statement.

Wray said: 'We've had a medical report on Miss Whittaker. Are you capable of listening?'

'Sure, go ahead.'

'It's not just a burglary. It's not an assault during the course of a burglary. She was raped.'

'That doesn't figure,' was Roach's immediate reaction.

'No, it doesn't, does it? Doesn't sound like Jackson's territory. So let's do this properly. I'm in charge now, but you're still on the case if you do what I tell you. We'll get what he's wearing. And you go and see Jackson's wife.'

'But we've agreed it couldn't be – '

120

'We haven't agreed anything. And we won't agree anything until we've got the facts and scrubbed round those that don't fit. So you'll see Jackson's wife and get his clothes from yesterday, and take them to forensic.'

'Either way she'll only cover his back.'

'So talk to her.' Wray's thin lips sketched a quite complimentary smile. 'You've got instinct, Ted, and that's good. But right now we'll get down to sorting this out scientifically.'

Ted Roach was not sure that the dispassionate scientific approach was the sort of thing that would cut much ice with Shena Jackson. Nor did he think she would exactly welcome his request for Terry's suit and shirt and underpants. But if that was what Wray wanted, he would get it; and maybe one fine day he would listen to a lecture about the gut reaction approach rather than the scientific stuff. Maybe.

Roach set off towards the Jackson house, followed by a car with a police forensic officer.

Outside the house was Jackson's rusty blue car. They prowled round it, and Roach tried the boot. It opened easily enough. The state of the bodywork was so ragged that you could almost have prized the whole vehicle apart with your bare hands. He waved into the murky depths of the boot. 'You're looking for traces of garden materials. Anything to do with garden rubbish. He said he took rose clippings, and wood, pieces of a chair. That's for elimination. For real evidence, any traces of cloth, hair, blood. Let me know, will you?'

He left the forensic officer to it and headed for the house. At the front door he hesitated with his finger on the bell-push, then walked round the side and through the gate in a garden trellis.

Shena Jackson and her younger daughter were hanging out washing. From an open upstairs window there came the thump and boom of a pop record. The girl was laughing about something, and her mother tried to smile back; but the lines

121

of her face were tired and worn, not accustomed to much happiness in recent years.

The two of them became aware of Ted Roach at the same time, and were suddenly silent. Shena went on pegging up a pullover and two blouses. Not until Roach was standing right beside her did she admit he was there.

She said: 'I phoned the UB office. He can sign on before they close. They were very helpful.'

'I'm afraid it won't be that soon, Shena.'

She brushed aside a skirt that had blown back in her face. 'You want some sort of statement? Mind if I finish hanging this lot up?'

Roach knew she was playing for time, putting off what she already sensed was going to be an evil moment. 'Shena, it's a bit more serious this time.'

'Has he finally thumped one of you?'

'Can someone look after Claire?'

Shena said resignedly: 'Sally's in.' She nodded towards the upstairs window. Sally was leaning on the sill, looking down with a very serious expression. Roach started to wave, then held back.

The moment they were indoors Shena found another way of stalling, insisting it was time she had a cup of coffee, and it wouldn't take a minute, and Ted could make himself comfy in the sitting-room. When the mugs of coffee were steaming between them and there were no more possible postponements, she sat and waited for the worst.

'How's he been, recently?' asked Roach. 'His behaviour?'

'How d'you mean?'

'Happy? Sad?'

She shrugged. 'Terry.'

'The usual.'

'Lazy sod.'

'Have you been talking okay?'

'Talking?' she said ruefully. 'We're married.'

'Any difference . . . moodiness . . . ?'

122

'I just cook and wash up. I don't notice anything.' She hesitated. 'Since he got out last he's been knocking back the drink a bit.'

'What about last night?'

'Oh, Ted, what do you expect me to – '

'There's somebody else involved, Shena.' It was time to stop the pussyfooting and let her have it. 'A girl.'

'Terry? She's welcome to him.'

'She was in bed, asleep, and heard someone in the flat.' She was trying to look indifferent, but it wasn't working. Roach said forcefully: 'I want the clothes he wore last night.'

'Underpants and vest. That's what he sleeps in these days, I think.'

'You think?'

She was trying to play it with her old brassy perkiness. 'You get past that sort of thing, don't you?'

'You don't sleep together now?' He still did not believe it could have been Terry Jackson – not the Terry Jackson he had known over the years – but if there was nothing doing with his wife, if he was frustrated and it was all building up inside him, then maybe after all . . . He said: 'Shena, you've always covered for him and I respect that. But look, I'm not saying this is Terry, all right? I don't want to say it's Terry.'

She was staring at him, hiding fear with contempt. 'Just what are you trying to put across?'

'This girl in the flat,' said Roach slowly and remorselessly, 'She came downstairs and found him there and screamed.'

'Bit much, wasn't it?'

'Not everyone's used to being burgled. Not yet. Whoever it was, he grabbed her. Fair enough, she was making a noise. But then he got friendly, if that's the right way to put it. She's about twenty-one, twenty-two, a really nice girl. She *was* nice. He raped her, Shena.' He waited, then prompted: 'Shena? I want those – '

'You're too late,' she rasped out. 'They're washed and on

123

the line, right? They're no use to you. So just get out of here, Ted.'

The doctor was far from happy that Jennifer Whittaker should have been persuaded to sign the necessary forms and discharge herself from hospital. He looked with frank disfavour on Ackland and Hollis when they came in to report that the car was waiting. Whatever the police wanted, he was convinced it would not be in the patient's interest. But she had agreed to leave, so that was that.

'We can't force her, can we?' he said ironically.

Tosh Lines was at the wheel of the car. He got out to open the passenger door as June Ackland carefully steered Jenny down the steps. The girl, wincing slightly as she reached street level, looked pale but determined.

She did not say a word as Lines drove more slowly and carefully than usual through the streets to Sun Hill, and did not once appear to look out of the window at the jostling, everyday world outside. When they arrived in the station yard she got out unaided, and straightened up as DCI Wray came to meet them.

'Miss Whittaker. It's very good of you to be so helpful.'

She spoke very levelly and distinctly, rather like someone who had memorized a lesson and could not depart from one word or phrase of it without losing the thread entirely. 'I couldn't face talking to just anyone in your place. It wouldn't be any help to you, I can tell you that. I want to see Mr Roach – detective sergeant, yes? I hope that will be all right. It's what I want.'

Wray, taken by surprise, did not show it by more than a momentary hesitation. Then he nodded to Ackland to take Jenny Whittaker inside to an interview room while he went off in search of Roach.

It was a quiet afternoon at Sun Hill. For once there were no feet pounding along the corridor outside the door, or up and down the echoing staircase. No drunks or arrested demonstrators were kicking up hell in the custody area, determined to make themselves heard from here to the Houses of Parliament. Jenny folded her hands in her lap. She looked a very ordinary, well-brought-up girl, pretty but not blatantly so: used to a pleasant, ordinary life, never dreaming of what had happened to her last night. Things like that only happened in the newspapers, to other people. It was a few minutes before she broke the silence.

'What do they say it's like – other victims, giving evidence?'

'We can't convict if people *don't* give evidence. You just have to say what's happened.'

'I'm not sure how I'll manage. I can't even think about it.'

To Ackland's relief, the door opened and Ted Roach came in. He looked angry about something, but the moment he saw Jenny he forced himself to calm down and offer her a reassuring smile. 'Have they been looking after you all right?'

She looked keen to smile back, and nod, and show she trusted him. 'They were very kind at the hospital, but I discharged myself.' Instead of waiting for further reassurance from him, she helped him out with the matter he was nerving himself to raise. 'The word you're looking for,' she said, 'is rape.'

'I'd like to ask you some questions.'

She managed another sketch of a smile. 'Well, there's nothing here to throw at you, so – '

'We've arrested a suspect.'

Jenny went very still. 'Where is he?'

'He's here. In this station.'

'Where in the station?' she breathed.

'Locked up.'

'So was I. Locked up. Front door, deadlock and chain. He got through that without too much trouble. All right, you can say I'm being hysterical. But I don't feel very safe anywhere.'

'That's natural.'

'I never thought of myself as a victim. I suppose nobody
125

does until it actually hits them.' She took a deep breath. 'What are you going to do with him?'

'We've got some evidence. I've got a feeling he might be ready to confess, but . . . first of all, could you identify him?'

Jenny nodded. 'And then what?'

'Jenny, you've trusted me, haven't you?'

'So far.'

'And I haven't let you down.'

'If I said "not yet", would you mind? I don't know if I trust anybody very much at the moment.'

'It means giving evidence in Court,' he said flatly.

'And what's that like? What do other victims say?' she asked again.

It was Roach's turn to look apprehensive. He had to tell her the truth. With Jenny Whittaker it would be fatal, now, to do otherwise. He said: 'Some of them say it's like being raped again.'

There was a tap at the door, and Hollis put his head round. Roach glared.

'Sorry, sarge, but you're wanted.'

Roach looked at Jenny. She nodded quite calmly, and turned to talk to June Ackland.

In the corridor, Hollis said importantly, as though he had been solely responsible for making an important collar: 'It's Mrs Jackson. You know, Shena Jackson. In front office.'

Sergeant Tom Penny was glad of something to occupy him the moment he arrived. Grimly he had gone through the motions of booking Terry Jackson in, reciting his rights to him, and agreeing to send for a solicitor. Last time it had been Mulgrove. The man hadn't done Jackson much good then, but he had no other names to trot out, so Mulgrove it would have to be again. Penny had seen Brownlow only fleetingly, and knew there was more to come. The more he could concentrate on familiar routines, the longer he could postpone the real roasting. If this present business could be made to last

126

long enough, Brownlow might go home – he never had been keen on overtime for himself – and the interview could wait until tomorrow.

Not that it would be any pleasanter tomorrow.

Penny turned his attention to the job in hand. He and Lines went to Jackson's cell. It gave Penny a certain satisfaction to see somebody in far worse trouble than himself. He held out a paper boiler suit.

'Get changed into this.'

'Where's my solicitor?'

'On his way.'

'I want him right this minute.'

'We know he's clever, Terry,' said Tosh Lines, 'but he can't fly. Not yet, anyway.'

They gave Jackson ten minutes, then led the police surgeon to the cell. When he had introduced himself, Jackson began to bluster.

'I don't get this. I'm perfectly all right. Don't need any surgeon or any other kind of medic.'

'I need to take samples.'

'Samples? What you on about?'

'Certain items may require some consent,' said the surgeon patiently. 'Others don't. It'll be better if you come with me to the medical room.'

'Not without Mr Mulgrove.'

The surgeon looked an enquiry at Sergeant Penny. Obviously it would save a lot of hassle if the solicitor could be present, or at least informed of exactly what was going on.

They did not have long to wait. Mulgrove bustled in with an aura of self-importance and of harassment. He was a busy man in his late forties, working hard to inch his way up the ladder out of reach of petty criminals and on to the really big stuff. At the desk he was greeted by Lines, questioned him and Sergeant Penny on the basic charges, but brushed them aside the moment he spotted DCI Wray. He switched at once to a display of respect for Wray's seniority, with the implication that the two of them were likely to share civilized doubt about the motives of his underlings.

'Let's face it, from what I can gather you really have very little against my client. Except perhaps a few old grudges.'

'We shall be interviewing Jackson again very shortly. And he is anxious that you shall be present at the next stage.'

'I should think so. It all sounds a little threadbare to me. Articles found in a sack . . . And a lot of people use that place to dump. It's blameworthy, but hardly criminal. Are we talking about burglary,' asked Mulgrove pedantically, 'or handling?'

'We're talking about rape.'

Ted Roach, leading Mrs Jackson from the front desk towards a vacant interview room, glanced briefly at the solicitor with a curl of the lip.

Ten

This time Roach made no pretence of matiness. He did not try to set Shena at her ease or look encouraging, but simply sat waiting for her to come out with whatever it was that had brought her here.

She took a plastic carrier bag out of her bulging black shopping bag and handed it over. 'Cigarettes,' she explained. 'Chocolate, an apple, orange.'

'Okay.' He did not question it. Shena was not the kind to try smuggling in a file or a flick-knife or anything that melodramatic. 'Do you want to see him?'

She shook her head violently. 'Look, do you know what it's like? Sally's in secondary school now. I can't hide the papers from her any more. Every time Terry's reported in one of them – '

'There are plenty of Jacksons.'

'They print the address these days.'

'Nothing we can do to stop that.'

She had difficulty in getting the next words out. 'What's her . . . what's the girl's name?'

'Jennifer.'

'Is she all right?'

So Shena believed in the girl now. And might believe a lot that she couldn't have accepted at first. Given time to think, her instinctive rejection of the idea had faded. On top of everything else he had done to her and his family, her husband had now been mixed up with another woman. A younger woman. Very nastily mixed up.

Roach said: 'We haven't got much time, Shena. I'm supposed to be interviewing him again, right this minute.'

'Oh, no.' There was a flash of her old defiance. 'Things to do. People to nick. Don't forget they're people, Ted.'

Thanks for reminding me, he thought wryly. But he tried to stay cool and attentive. The others waiting for him would have to wait. Shena had come here for something more than just handing over cigarettes and a few things for her husband to chew on.

'He *has* been different.' She was answering the question he had asked all those hours ago. 'I hadn't noticed it really. Too busy. Well, I had noticed, but I didn't think about it.'

She looked wretchedly at him. All the accumulation of the years with Terry and the long periods without him, when he was in prison, came up in a dark, swirling tide behind her eyes. Roach could read her thoughts; could almost smell her memories. He knew the hopeless world she had had to walk through. Even when Terry had served his time and was out again, how could she forget? In memory she would always see those visiting rooms; every time she watched a television play or documentary showing the slop buckets, the iron stairs and the iron faces of the screws, and the filth, she would be back there. She would never be free from the places that Terry's activities had forced her to take Sally and Claire to, every two weeks. Giving your name at the gates, and then at last meeting Terry in his greys, pale and tired. Caged. And what would the two girls, silent and scared, make of it all?

Each time he came out it would be just that much worse. Roach knew the symptoms. Freedom could be frightening: something a man lost the ability to cope with. After a few spells inside, no man could ever be at ease walking the streets, playing with the kids in the park, helping his wife carry the shopping home.

Roach throttled down his sympathy. There was still something she had to tell him.

'After that last time I couldn't let him touch me,' she was

saying. 'I tried, you know, but . . . it was no good. So Terry, he got moody. Angry sometimes. Not so much with us, or me, but with himself. He couldn't change the way it always was. I married him because I thought he was strong. But he isn't. Any silly little temptation, and he's away. He's weak against himself, and that's as weak as any man ever gets.'

'Shena . . .'

She looked slowly down at her shopping bag and after a moment's wondering silence lifted it as if it were an almost unmanageable weight. 'Maybe you can help him.' She made up her mind, and dug down into the bag. 'There's another bundle in here. It's his clothes. I . . . it wasn't true, what I said. He hadn't given them to me to wash. And there's blood on them.'

He escorted her back to the reception area and out of the main door. It would have been insulting to offer her any cheap words of comfort. He tried simply to touch her arm, but having gone through with delivering the damning contents of the bag she wanted no more to do with him. Wrenching her arm away, she walked steadily down the road towards the bus stop without once glancing back.

Roach took the clothes through the custody area to the cupboard where they kept specimen bags. He was writing a label when Ackland came through.

'Sarge, do you – '

'Take this to the lab, will you,' he interrupted. 'I need it quickly.'

'Did you want to speak to Miss Whittaker again?'

'No.' As she moved away, he said hastily: 'June, tell her thanks.'

'Are you okay?'

'I'll let you know if I've got any problems, June.'

No problems left, right now. He ought to feel fine. Jubilant over a good job well done. Damn it, he did feel fine. It was a great sensation, knowing you'd sorted things out, got the pieces to fit and made sure the whole thing was watertight.

That was what this job was all about. At the same time there was this sickness in the stomach that he had to fight down. A petty thief like Terry Jackson was one thing: all so easy and straightforward. You knew where you were with those little creeps and could actually get to like them, more often than not. You might almost say it was the existence of small-time villains like Terry that kept policemen in their job. But for Jackson to turn like this, become something so foul and stinking, threw everything off balance.

Don't forget they're people . . .

And that included Jennifer Whittaker. Jackson didn't seem to have let that stop him.

Roach moved on towards the main interview room. This was going to be it.

As he opened the door, Jackson's solicitor was uttering one of his repertoire of ritual complaints. 'How long is this farce going to take? It's ridiculous, utterly ridiculous.'

Roach went straight to the recording machine, switched it on, announced the date and time, and gabbled: 'Interview between Detective Sergeant Roach and Terence Andrew Jackson, attended by James Mulgrove, solicitor, and Detective Constable Lines.' He seated himself. 'Right, Terry.'

Jackson looked pathetically vulnerable in his paper boiler suit. It was hardly fair to harass a man already humiliated in this way. But Roach was not interested in being fair. All he wanted was to slam the truth home and get a result without any more lying and evasions.

'Terry, would you tell us in your own words what you were doing at two o'clock this morning.' When Jackson glanced at his solicitor, Roach raised his voice. 'Come on. If you were sleeping, say you were sleeping.'

'I've been told to say nothing, Ted.'

'No-one's told you anything. Your solicitor's advised you, that's what he does. It's up to you. It's still up to you, Terry.'

'No, I'll do what he says.' Jackson shifted awkwardly, and his paper clothing crackled.

132

'Oh, don't be silly. If you're innocent, say so. It doesn't make any difference to me. I'll just go off and find out who did do it. Terry, for your own sake wake up, you're in it up to your ears.'

'Duress,' Mulgrove protested.

'I apologize.' Roach quietened down; tried to make it sound chatty and informal, inviting the suspect to share his own easygoing cynicism. 'Come on, Terry. Your wife's just been in with the clothes you wore. She's dumped you.'

Mulgrove seized the opportunity to be outraged.

'Terminate this interview. I'd like to have a word with my client.'

Roach nodded to Tosh Lines to switch off the tape. There was a silence. Having made his demand, Mulgrove now looked unsure of himself.

'Go on,' Roach invited. 'Don't let me stop you.'

Mulgrove made up his mind. 'All right. My client is prepared . . .' He silently consulted Jackson, who managed a nod. 'Prepared,' said Mulgrove, 'to admit to burglary. But we'll contest the charge of rape. Vigorously.'

Roach knew perfectly well what that meant. If the police did not lay off the rape, Jackson's brief would give Jennifer Whittaker hell in the witness box. He had seen it done before, and knew the effect it would have on Jenny. A good counsel – if you could describe one using tactics like that as good – seized every opportunity of implying that the victim was no better than she should be, and even that she rather enjoyed a bit of a rough and tumble. But there was no turning back now. And no deals.

When the tape was spooling again, he said: 'Interview recommenced. Persons present as before.' He stared steadily at Terry Jackson. 'Shena's dropped you. Everybody's dropped you. You're on your own. So what happened?' Jackson tried to look away, but there was no way Roach's gaze would let him escape. 'You watched the flat for a couple of nights, took it for empty. Right so far?'

'Ted . . .'

'Is that right so far?' And impatiently, when Jackson tried a mute appeal to Mulgrove, 'Terry, it's down to you.'

'I'm not saying anything. All right, so I did the burglary, but that's the lot. I left it quietly, Ted, I swear to God.'

'Hold on. I've asked you this a few times. It's important. Because I need to be sure. If there's somebody else out there on the loose . . .' He let the implication hang in the air. 'Okay, then. Why did you dump the stuff so fast? What made you panic?'

'I only did the burglary,' whined Jackson. 'I didn't touch her. I didn't want to, I . . .' He shuddered to a stop, scared by what he had just heard himself say.

'You what?'

'I only did the burglary. That's all. Why don't you listen to me? You won't get off me. I can't shake you bastards off me.'

He wiped a paper sleeve across his eyes.

Roach said: 'We're still here, Terry.'

Terry Jackson's shoulders slumped. 'I . . . I didn't want to hurt her. You've got to believe me. I didn't hurt her, really.' It was a last appeal, a last attempt at a denial. But even Mulgrove's face showed that it wasn't going to work. Defeated, he slumped back and made no further attempt to halt his client.

Now it all came out. After Jenny had stopped shouting, Jackson had got scared. She wouldn't listen to him. He wanted to talk, that was all. Somehow he never got the chance of just talking any more. She was so young. And Roach remembered what Shena had said about the smells and the filth, and how Terry had drawn in on himself. Contaminated by those wasted years, he must have felt filthy, felt ugly, so close to that nice, frightened, attractive girl. He hadn't wanted her to be frightened. He kept saying that. He had tried to tell her everything was all right. He just needed money, clothes for the kids. He had actually told her about the kids, but she wasn't capable of listening. He wanted to hold her, rock her

134

to sleep, tell her it was all right. He wouldn't hurt her. He was only Terry, Terry Jackson. Terry was okay, nothing to be frightened of. But now, in this room, Terry himself was frightened. He looked at Ted Roach, knowing he was gone beyond all hope now. 'Oh God, Ted, I didn't mean it.'

All that was left today was to bring the paperwork up to date. The cost of nicking somebody nowadays must be in the region of five acres of rain forest. Roach plodded away, ignoring Tosh Lines's offer of a reviving drink across the road. That would have to wait until much later. And he wasn't so sure it would revive him.

June Ackland, on her way off duty, put her head round the door. She was rather smartly dressed. It was not inconceivable that DCI Wray was waiting not far away in his car. 'Sarge, Jenny Whittaker wanted me to pass on her thanks.'

'All in a day's work,' he said gruffly.

'And sarge, I'm sorry if . . . that is . . .'

'If what? You didn't trust me? Did you think I'd bully her? She talked, I didn't need to.'

'You handled it – '

He was too tetchy to let her finish. 'I did my job, that's all. Listen, if you let it get to you, you're finished. I learnt that a long time ago. Victim, suspect, evidence, charge. That's all it is. They're not people to me, they're bits of paper, lots of bits of paper.'

She smiled, and for a moment he envied Gordon Wray. But that smile made it plain that she did not believe him. And he was sneakily unsure that he himself believed it.

The hell with it. Maybe he did need that drink after all.

Just one, before going home. Just one. Not like that flaming lunatic Tom Penny.

Eleven

Morning parade was overshadowed by the cloud that everyone knew was settling down over Sergeant Tom Penny's
head. It was not that Penny had been highly thought of by
any of the reliefs. He was probably the least popular sergeant
in the place. Yet he had become part of the scenery: he was
one of the team, there at predictable times and behaving in
the way you were accustomed to his behaving. His temporary
replacement, Sergeant Corrie, was untried; and his lack of
familiarity with the officers on the relief showed up all too
clearly. It created a feeling of instability, which was the last
thing they needed when going out on patrol.

'Er, so that's Hollis in Panda Two. And . . .' Corrie floun-
dered. 'Oh, yes. Quinnan, Beat Five.'

'Right, skip.' Dave Quinnan contrived to make his cheerful
acceptance sound derisive.

'Stamp and Young . . .' Corrie looked up from his clip-
board. 'Which is Young?'

'Me, skip.'

'Station duties. Right, that's it. Have a good one.' He was
all too genuinely anxious to be regarded as one of the lads.

The general consensus was that he wouldn't last. But there
would have to be somebody, sooner or later, to step into
Penny's shoes. It would be funny without Penny doing his
little pieces around the place. Now that he was for the chop,
everybody suddenly wished him well, and even wished he
could stay on. The last thing anyone wanted in this job was
a personnel upheaval.

'Gets done today, doesn't he?' said Stamp on the way out.

136

'That's right.' Reg Hollis looked sorrowful, as he invariably did when enjoying a gloat over some fresh disaster.

'We'll miss the miserable old git.'

'I think maybe I should drop in on him,' said Hollis, 'and tell him his rights.'

'That'll cheer him up no end.'

Unease was not confined to the relief. In Chief Superintendent Brownlow's conference room he held back Chief Inspector Conway at the end of what he always referred to, with his practised twinkle, as morning prayers. Conway guessed what was coming, on this day of all days.

He was right. 'Tom Penny,' said Brownlow.

Conway was ready for it. He had had a quiet word, but the most he could achieve was to ensure that the case went in at the end of the list. There would be a minimal chance of adverse publicity. All the folk who ought to know had been informed. The Complaints Chief Inspector would be there with his scribe. The sooner the whole sorry business was settled, the better. A lot depended on how philosophical Tom Penny was going to be in that regard.

'Someone should have a word with him,' suggested Brownlow. 'Express our sympathy, let him know our thoughts are with him.'

'Mm,' was the most Conway could manage.

'It would also be helpful to sound him out – tactfully, of course – about his plans in the event of a conviction.'

'Which,' Conway pointed out, 'is inevitable, short of a miracle.'

'Yes. Well, see if you can fit in a visit later this morning.'

'Me?'

'Yes, Derek.'

None of it was really worth the effort. It was far too late now to undo the damage that had been done. Fine words would be as useless as hard words. Nevertheless in the upper ranks and the lower ranks there was a feeling of resentment. None of it need have happened without the vengeful gang

137

from Barton Street. Exposing their crooked sergeant had been a public duty. But with Penny you weren't talking about villainy. Slightly too much alcohol in the blood, all right. But no damage, no accident, nothing. If he had been a lorry driver he might have lost his HGV licence for a set period, but he could have gone back to it afterwards. Here was a man's whole career down the tubes.

Stamp turned on Hollis, who had always set himself up as the official Federation complaints purveyor – voice of the downtrodden masses, as Stamp himself had been known to call him. What was their spokesman doing on Penny's behalf?

Hollis could not restrain himself from looking smug. 'As a matter of fact, I have decided to consult with the unfortunate officer this very morning.'

'What d'you suppose he'll do?'

'As you'll understand' – Hollis was in his element – 'it will be in the nature of a confidential consultation between the accused party and his advisor.'

'Don't be a ponce, Reg. What d'you suppose he'll do – put his hands up?'

'If you ask me,' contributed Loxton, 'I'd say he's got good convincing grounds for pleading not guilty by reason of insanity.'

Tom Penny had braced himself for what was undoubtedly going to be the most miserable day of his whole life. It had been bad enough not getting the commendation he had been entitled to. To be dragged through the dirt and be condemned in the eyes of the whole public and robbed of any chance of ever again having a stab at the promotion he had been waiting for so long was ten times worse. But he was not going to go down without one hell of a fight. He'd give the whole crowd of them something to think about. In front of his shaving mirror he had already prepared the outline of his defence.

There were certain aspects of the background to the case which he felt ought to be brought out into the light of day.

His chin jutted combatively as he thought about it. Every one of his own colleagues would vouch that some time prior to the incident in question he had been instrumental in exposing a corrupt and violent police officer. That man had been a colleague of the very officers who stopped him on the night in question. Far from being the perpetrator of a crime, he, Sergeant Thomas Penny, was in fact the victim of a criminal conspiracy.

'The innocent victim of a criminal conspiracy,' he stressed aloud.

Then, shaven and neatly dressed and ready for battle, he went first to see his doctor. He had promised both his wife and Brownlow that he would do this. He knew exactly what they both wanted. He would honour his promise, but he was not going to give in to what he was sure had already been set up: set up not to help him, but to save everybody else's face. He had had enough of other people's faces, not to mention their interfering voices: Bob Cryer meaning well but talking crap; Brownlow waffling away with his usual load of hypocritical generalizations; and Wendy, worried about his pension and the housekeeping money and everything except his pride and what was due to him.

Dr Cunningham went through the usual procedures, for all the difference they could possibly make. Blood pressure, heart, lungs, knee jerks, the lot. His conclusions were pretty obvious.

'Stress isn't like chickenpox. I can't say it's cleared up, because it doesn't necessarily show. But in any ordinary way you're fit now. It's a matter of whether you yourself feel able to cope.'

'I didn't come here for psychiatric social work, thanks. Am I officially still signed off sick, or not?'

'If you're not fit for work,' Cunningham suggested obliquely, 'you're not fit to stand trial.'

It occurred grimly to Penny that in the old days a man had to be certified healthy before he could be hanged. He saw no

139

reason why he should dodge the issue. He wanted this whole business over and done with.

'Put me down as fit and well.'

'That's your choice.' The doctor pulled a form towards him and reached for his pen. 'I also want you to think about the future.'

'Yes, that'll really keep me cheerful.'

'I mean after the trial. In my opinion you've never fully recovered from the shock and stress of that gunshot injury. If it comes to it, I'll be quite willing to write to your chief medical officer recommending that you be allowed to resign on medical grounds.'

'Now you're talking like Bob bloody Cryer. Put me in the waste bin with no embarrassment for the job. That's the idea, isn't it?'

He drove home fuming. As he parked the car he realized that this might be the last occasion for some time on which he would be legally allowed to drive. Never a scrape, never an accident; and yet he was in danger of being banned from the roads. And Wendy, who had shoved up their insurance by three stupid accidents in four years, would be legally permitted to drive him around.

He had not been indoors five minutes when the front door bell rang, and he heard an all too familiar voice along the hall.

'Mrs Penny? Reg Hollis, colleague of your husband's. He's probably mentioned me.'

'No, I don't think so.'

It would take more than that to abash Hollis. 'Well, anyway, could I have a word with him?'

If Penny could have foreseen such a visitation, he would have warned Wendy in advance not to let the miserable little oick across the doormat. But it was too late. She was even suggesting a cup of tea or coffee as she brought him towards the sitting-room.

'I'm sure Tom'll be wanting one. He's only just got back from the doctor's.'

140

'Oh?' Trust Hollis to be so quick with the guesswork. 'A terrible thing, stress. My God, I should know, I've gone through plenty of it myself.' As he was shown into the room, he beamed encouragingly. 'Morning, skipper. Good to see you.'

'What do you want?'

Hollis glanced uncertainly at Wendy. 'Just a chat, see how you're getting on. All the boys and girls at the station have been asking.'

Penny's glance sent his wife sliding out of the room, not renewing the offer of a cup of tea.

When the door had closed behind her, Penny snapped: 'Who sent you, Hollis?'

'No, no, skip, you've got the wrong idea. Not like that at all. I'm here off my own bat, to see if you'd like me to be your friend.'

Penny was incredulous. The idea of ever seeking any friendship from Hollis, with that sly drooping face and the shiftiness of his left eye, which seemed to work independently of the right one, was too wild and way out. Today had started out badly and was steadily getting worse.

'In the technical sense, of course,' Hollis was going eagerly on. 'You're entitled to have a Friend, as they put it, representing and advising you at the inquiry.'

'What inquiry?'

'Disciplinary. Into your criminal conviction.'

'I haven't been tried yet, Hollis.'

'No, fair point, but I mean . . . well, we all know, driving over the limit . . . it's pretty much open and shut, isn't it?'

'Is it?'

'Well, I don't have to tell you, do I? How many get off these days since they got the intoximeter teething troubles sorted out?'

Tom Penny felt that if he did not immediately get PC Hollis off the premises, it was Hollis who would be conscious of some troubles with his teeth. A selection of them on the sitting-room carpet would relieve Penny's feelings considerably. He got up and held the door open.

'Thank you for your interest, Hollis. I won't keep you from your duties. I'm sure you ought to be halfway round the dicier bits of the Jasmine Allan estate by now.'

In the doorway, Hollis persisted. 'Naturally you need a while to think about it. But I'd be happy to make myself available as your representative. Being a Federation man, I've had a lot of experience of . . . well, you know . . .' He shrugged knowledgeably.

Penny had to push past him along the passage in order to get to the front door and heave it open. 'Can I speak frankly, man to man?'

'Certainly. That's my whole point. Feel free.'

'Sod off. If I need a representative – a *Friend* – I'll choose one appropriate to my rank and experience in the Force.'

'You're under a lot of pressure, skip, I can see that, so I won't take offence,' said Hollis magnanimously. He paused on the step. 'But the offer still holds. If you need my help – '

'I'll jump in front of a tube train.'

Penny slammed the front door and stormed back to the sitting-room. In his head he began going over and over each phrase and inflection of his defence speech again, for what must be the ninth or tenth time. He could not bear to sit down for more than a few moments. He was pacing up and down, starting to declaim a few telling lines and pounding them home with a clenched fist, when there was another ring at the doorbell.

They were not going to leave him alone. He would be hoarse before he even got to Court.

This time it was Chief Inspector Conway, in civvies. He looked grim, dourly going through with his duty and not even attempting the smarmy goodfellowship of a Hollis; but this time Penny asked Wendy to bring in some coffee.

'Sit down, sir.'

'No uniform, no ranks, Tom.' Without his uniform, though,

Conway looked uncomfortable and out of place. 'I wanted to talk to you man to man.'

'As bad as that, is it?' Penny had no intention of making it easy for his visitor. Condescension, pity, or bullying: they were all the same thing now, and could make no difference to the outcome.

Everything had gone wrong. Reg Hollis busting his way in, Conway paying a call: it was new, and all wrong. He looked round the room, at the photograph frame with the fading picture of himself and Wendy in it, hardly ever looked at and certainly never sentimentalized over these days, but an integral part of the place. Like the television, and the drinks cabinet with a chip in a corner of the door mirror that they were always going to have replaced but had never got round to. And Wendy's untidy heap of women's magazines, which she half-read and then dumped on the nearest flat surface. It was his private world, not shared with the offices and corridors of Sun Hill, not linked in any way. Yet now they were coming here from the nick, faces he saw every day but not in these surroundings. It was the wrong background. Vibrations of Sun Hill were quivering in through every crack, invading his home and giving it quite the wrong sound, smell and feeling.

Conway said: 'It goes without saying that everybody at Sun Hill feels totally gutted on your behalf, Tom. I hope you know that.'

Oh, he could guess that all right. A genuine shiver of 'There but for the grace of God . . .' He had felt it himself enough times in the past. But as well as that there was a desire now to hush it up, rush it through and make sure he didn't say anything out of turn. If a chief inspector had come to set foot in the Penny home, it wasn't for any sociable, comradely feeling.

'The circumstances,' Conway was intoning, 'were particularly . . . uh . . . regrettable.'

'Regrettable? I was the victim of a criminal conspiracy.'

Wendy brought in a tray with two cups of instant coffee,

143

milk, sugar, and a plate of biscuits. She glanced from her husband to the chief inspector, and went despondently out. When Conway picked up his cup and very slowly stirred sugar into it, it was easy to see that he was trying to find the right, mollifying thing to say. That was what he had been sent here for. It was equally easy to guess who had sent him. Pop round and have a word with him, make sure he's going to do the decent thing. All too obvious. But the truth behind it was all too obvious as well. Brownlow and the rest of them couldn't help but know it. He had reported a Barton Street officer for assaulting a prisoner. That officer was subsequently shown to be corrupt. Nobody could deny that. And nobody in his right mind would doubt that Barton Street officers had put him in the frame as an act of revenge.

Conway went on stirring his coffee. 'Tom, you were stopped for a moving traffic offence. You were breathalysed. You were over the limit. You're guilty.'

'That's the official version, eh? All neat and tidy, get rid of the rotten apple, and everything in the garden will be lovely.'

'Nobody's happy about this. But Tom, whatever you feel right now, do give serious, sensible thought to what will happen after the trial.'

'Because you've all made up your minds I'm guilty.'

Always on a short fuse, Conway was already close to losing control of his temper. His thin, pale lips tightened, and his voice became more like his usual harsh, domineering bark. 'It doesn't matter if *we* think you're Lord Lucan or Shirley Temple. There'll be a chief inspector and his bagman from Complaints at the trial. If you're convicted there'll have to be an inquiry, and you will be required to resign. There's no way any of us can stop that, and you know it.'

'If people could see the speed and enthusiasm with which police officers wash their hands,' said Penny bitterly, 'they'd never call us pigs.'

*

Reporting results to Brownlow was very rarely the easiest thing in the world. Brownlow always wanted to hear only what he wanted to hear. It had been left to Conway to make sure that Sergeant Penny did the decent thing and caused the minimum of trouble. The chief superintendent was in no mood to be told that Penny was in a mood for trouble. Sweet reason had never been Penny's forte.

Conway usually enjoyed the ambience of the golf club bar. Today he would have preferred to cut the lunchtime session short and get back to Sun Hill, waiting for the bad news to be brought in.

His temper was not soothed by his being kept waiting. Brownlow was deep in conversation near the window with a local builder. They laughed, made silly gestures, and then put their heads conspiratorially together. Looking at the builder's flushed face and the way he impatiently clicked his fingers at the club steward for another glass, Conway disloyally wondered how many times the man had driven his Jag back from the clubhouse when well over the limit; and what would have happened if he had come up in front of one of the three local magistrates who were members of this club and of other fraternal organizations. As one such himself, he had experienced these occasional flickers of moral unease; but could usually persuade them back into line.

When Brownlow deigned to come and join him, his good humour made it clear that he had played a successful round this morning. He had booked a table for the two of them to share a bar lunch, and when they were settled he listened to Conway's report without comment, but nodded understandingly as the CI concluded: 'Sorry I didn't get through to him, but he's never been an easy man to talk to at the best of times.'

'Resents attempts to help him.'

'More than one chip on his shoulder.'

'All the same, he must surely realize by now that there's

only one sensible way to handle this thing, in his own interests.'

'He knows it,' said Conway brusquely. 'Whether he'll act on it . . .'

The waitress set two microwaved plates of fish and croquette potatoes in front of them. 'Anything to drink, sir?'

'I think a glass of dry white wine would go down nicely.' It was a warm morning, and the idea of a cool glass of wine appealed to Conway also. Before he could nod acceptance of the expected invitation, however, Brownlow said: 'Oh, and a glass of orange juice for my colleague. He's driving.'

He smiled. Conway returned the smile with as much grace as he could muster.

If that was the way the boss wanted it, that was the way he would get it. When they left, Conway drove with exaggerated care. He did not pull away from lights until they had gone green, and stopped at zebra crossings when pedestrians were still trying to make up their minds whether or not to start out.

Brownlow's attention was caught by a flash of blue uniform in the crowds along a shopping street. He craned forward to have a good look as the car stopped at yet another set of lights. PC Quinnan was standing by the trays outside a greengrocer's shop, munching an apple. Conway glanced in the direction of Brownlow's gaze, to see Sergeant Corrie approaching and Quinnan hastily dropping the half-eaten apple and trying to kick it surreptitiously towards the gutter.

Brownlow allowed himself a chuckle. That really must have been a good round this morning.

'Corrie's making up "A" relief temporarily – that's so, isn't it?'

Conway nodded, keeping his eyes on the road. There was a clogged mess of parked cars on the corner, and getting round it could be dangerous if someone was coming too fast the other way. As he reached for the radio to bellow information and orders to Sun Hill, WPC Delia French bore down upon the congestion.

That should make their lives a misery.

'Good man, you think?' Brownlow was asking.

'Sir?'

'Corrie. What sort of an officer?'

'Oh, first-rate administrative skills, I think.'

'But he himself asked to get back on operational duties. Quite commendable. What would you think of him as a permanent replacement?'

Conway recalled the slightly unctuous way Sergeant Corrie had talked to himself and Inspector Monroe. There had been rather too much about the joys of getting back to shiftwork, leaving the desk and getting out on the beats, getting the feel of the ground again. 'Reading the streets,' had been one of his earnest phrases. 'Getting in amongst it, sir, where it's all happening.' Commendable, as Brownlow had said; but expressed a bit too dramatically for Conway's liking. Or Monroe's, come to that. Nor had they been too impressed by his keenness to keep in with the lads. Just a bit too sickly about playing fair with them and then they'd play fair with you: a smile, friendly word, pat on the back, working wonders. From experience both Monroe and Conway had learned to be more sceptical about the Sun Hill team spirit than that. He said:

'I think I'd want to see more of how he performs before deciding.'

'I'm sure that's wise. After all, if we are forced to lose Penny . . .'

Brownlow did not finish, but Conway knew what was in his mind and brutally finished it for him: 'We don't want to saddle ourselves with another passenger.'

Even in the privacy of the car, Brownlow did not want to endorse this blunt assessment too openly. Instead he glanced at his watch and changed the subject. 'Could you get a move on, Derek. I've got an appointment.'

147

'I'm doing what I can, sir,' said Conway with some relish, 'within the law.'

He halted at a zebra and courteously waved a crocodile of mixed infants across the road.

Twelve

At any rate one promise had been fulfilled. The hearing of Tom Penny's case had been pushed back to the end of the afternoon's proceedings. Not that this had been for his personal benefit. In some ways he would have preferred it to be earlier: get it over with, and not have to hang around the concourse of the magistrates' court avoiding other people's gaze, wondering if some of those waiting to be called had been petty criminals he had dealt with in the past. It would be a great day for them if any one of them recognized him as a fellow defendant instead of being a police witness.

He pretended to study the court lists and notices on the board at the side of the concourse.

Behind him, echoing faintly in the tiled chamber, he heard a familiar voice. Detective Sergeant Alastair Greig was greeting someone effusively. 'Hello there, guv'nor.'

It could hardly be Burnside. Penny risked a glance over his shoulder.

Two men had just come in through the swing doors, one of them carrying a briefcase. They were in civvies, but they were unmistakably policemen.

'Alastair Greig, right? It's been a few years now.'

They were shaking hands, Greig was being introduced and explaining that he was here with a committal for a fraud case. It had just been put back for the second time, and here they were getting near the end of the list. He could only hope it wasn't going to be postponed yet again.

'What brings you here from Barkingside? Not our usual Court, in the old days.'

'Oh, I'm not at Barkingside any longer,' said the older and heavier of the two men. 'I'm at the Dream Factory.'

'The Yard, eh?' Greig sounded impressed. It was just the kind of thing that would impress Greig and arouse his envy.

'Complaints.'

It must have dawned on Greig at the same moment it dawned on Penny. These two were here to record every detail of the charge against Penny, the verdict, and the details for the groundwork of an official inquiry. The executioners were on the premises even before a verdict had been delivered.

Penny heard Greig's footsteps clattering hastily away across the tiled, imitation mosaic floor. And he felt rather than heard the other two walk past him.

'Shouldn't take long,' the older man was saying, 'if everyone plays the game.'

Words swam through Penny's mind. He would speak out. No way was he going to surrender and let them walk over him, virtually wiping him out of existence.

A young man came crashing through the doors from the courtroom, tight-lipped but ready to explode the moment his solicitor had followed and the doors were closed behind them.

'I realize you're disappointed,' the solicitor was saying, 'but – '

'Pigs. Of course the bastard beak believed the lying bastard pigs, didn't he? A jury wouldn't have. We ought to have gone for a jury.'

He glared indiscriminately around, to find only Penny still waiting. Fortunately for himself, Penny was not recognizable as a policeman. The two men went out, the dissatisfied client's voice still audible as he stamped down the steps.

The Court PC was approaching. His tone of voice was both inquisitive and compassionate.

'You're on, mate. You know the drill.'

Yes, he knew the drill all right. Only this time he would be in the dock and not in the witness-box.

There were three magistrates on the bench. One was a

150

tight-lipped woman with a blue rinse which must have been specially organized this morning; another a hunched little man who surveyed the public seats over the tops of half-spectacles like a schoolmaster alert for any inattention or incipient trouble. The chairman was a balding ex-officer type with a neatly trimmed sandy moustache and a set expression of peppery impatience.

The PC led Penny to the dock and indicated the chair. In the well of the Court he could see Dewhurst and Tanner, each with a notepad open on his knee. *Whatever you say may be taken down and used in evidence* . . . This Court ordeal would not be the last ordeal he would have to undergo.

He'd tell them a thing or two.

The chairman leaned forward and conferred with the clerk, his manner suggesting that he was giving orders that they should all synchronize their watches and aim at finishing in five minutes flat.

At last they were ready. 'Stand up, Thomas Penny.'

Penny stood. He kept himself ramrod straight as the clerk began reading out a toneless liturgy which he must have used with very little variation a dozen times a day.

'Thomas Penny, you are charged that on the fifteenth of May 1991 at Wilsborough Street in this borough you drove a motor vehicle after consuming so much alcohol that the proportion in your breath exceeded the legal limit, contrary to section six of the Road Traffic Act 1972. How do you plead: guilty, or not guilty?'

Penny stared at the witness-box, wondering what he was doing here instead of being over there. He willed himself not to feel dizzy and fall over. He was on stage, and people were watching him, waiting for him to speak. But he was like an actor who found himself somehow in the wrong scene, at the wrong side of the stage; and he dried.

Below him he could see Dewhurst, studying him impassively. They were waiting, though, for his outburst. Penny tried to feel that in reality he was in charge here, the man

151

with the power over all of them. Let them scribble their notes about his defiance. Let them award him their black marks and dream up loads more accusations against him in the next stage of his persecution.

At last he swallowed, licked his lips, and said it: 'Guilty.'

He was allowed to sit down again.

Dewhurst glanced hopefully at his colleague.

The Crown Prosecution Service solicitor rose. 'The facts in this case are that on the night of fifteenth May 1991 Constables Wheeler and Alexander of Barton Street police station observed the accused driving a motor vehicle with a defective rear brake light. When they stopped the vehicle and questioned the accused, they found that his breath smelt of alcohol and asked him to submit to a breath test. When this proved positive he was taken to Barton Street police station, where the intoximeter reading showed that his blood alcohol level was one hundred and ten milligrams per hundred millilitres.'

The chairman conferred briefly with his colleagues. The woman gave Penny one contemptuous glare, and then did not look at him again. The man with the spectacles dabbed to and fro, his head pecking first towards the chairman and then down at some papers before him.

'Stand up.'

Penny got to his feet again.

The clerk said: 'Do you wish to address the Bench before sentence is pronounced?'

'Er . . . yes, yes, Your Worships.' It was all happening more quickly that he had anticipated. He fumbled in his pocket for the notes he had made, but when he unfolded the paper it seemed that the words had blurred, and he couldn't make head or tail of them. But he was not going to surrender. He raised his voice, trying for the authoritarian bluster so familiar to everyone at Sun Hill. 'Although I have pleaded guilty, there are certain aspects of the background to this case which I feel should be brought out into the light of day.' He was glad to see that this had shaken Dewhurst and his sidekick.

152

Serve them right. Dewhurst was staring, silently asking him what the hell he thought he was playing at. 'Er . . .'

And suddenly it had all collapsed again. He was at a loss. His notes were no help. He had forgotten the important bits that came next.

The Chairman prompted him curtly. 'Yes, Mr Penny?'

Penny shoved the notes back into his pocket. It was hopeless. 'I would just like to say' – he was surprised at his own calm – 'that I had been under considerable stress at the time of this incident. I have been receiving medical treatment over a long period. However this in no way excuses my foolish and irresponsible behaviour, which I deeply regret. It has never happened before and will not happen again.'

Dewhurst expelled an almost audible sigh of relief as Penny sat down.

Again the magistrates put their heads together. The Chairman seemed to making some point in mitigation, glancing with unexpected sympathy towards the accused, perhaps grateful for the swift ending of proceedings he had made possible. But the woman's blue hair nearly shook itself out of place, and the little man on the other side was jabbing his head across more and more forcefully. The two of them clearly belonged to that faction which believed all police officers should be incorruptible, non-smoking, teetotal eunuchs with haloes rather than helmets, spending their spare time singing in church choirs or attending meetings in temperance halls.

'Stand up.'

Once more Penny rose wearily. This was it.

The Chairman said: 'You are fined three hundred pounds and disqualified from driving for twelve months.'

Penny nodded. The Court PC was beckoning him to leave the dock.

In a dream he went out on to the concourse. It was almost deserted until Dewhurst and Tanner emerged. They made as if to talk to him, but he wasn't going to be either patronized or lectured. He hurried off at a tangent, only to run straight

153

into somebody else he knew and could have done without. It was Alastair Greig again, appearing from a side door with a bulging document case and an evening paper under his arm.

'Tom!' Greig looked momentarily uneasy, but made it sound as if there was nobody else he would sooner have encountered at this moment.

'You still here?'

'Wrapping up a few details on that infernal postponed case next door.' Greig kept it breezy. 'And how did things go with you?'

'How the hell do you think they went?'

'Sure, silly thing to say.' Greig glanced at his watch. 'Look . . . uh . . . why don't we nip across the road and have a quick cup of tea?'

'For God's sake leave me alone.'

Penny pushed past him and went unsteadily down the steps to the street.

Sergeant Corrie was enjoying himself. It was great to be out in the open air after these recent years at a desk. They had made it plain to him that he had a good career ahead of him on the admin side – lots of officers would jump at the opportunities offered – but he had hankered for a return to the real job and contact with real people. He prided himself on being a good mixer, at ease with the public and strict but fair with the men and women on his relief. He would soon build up a healthy relationship with this new team.

Yesterday he had paced the streets to get his bearings in the neighbourhood, had a useful chat with PC Quinnan, and been introduced to the local greengrocer; though perhaps later he ought to warn Quinnan that, while a spirit of co-operation between police and local tradesmen was to be encouraged, it ought not to become too friendly. Personal relationships could prove embarrassing if it ever became necessary to take official action involving the tradesman concerned. He thought that

154

PC Quinnan was the sort of conscientious officer who would welcome a friendly word of advice.

Today Corrie was out with PC Hollis in a Panda car. Hollis seemed a useful contact. As Federation representative at Sun Hill, he was obviously deeply involved with his colleagues' welfare, and although Corrie had no intention of prying, it would do no harm to get a few personal pointers to broaden his knowledge of the team.

This was another morning when he was glad to be out of the nick, though for a different reason. The news about Tom Penny's appearance in Court yesterday and the sentence had really put the mockers on the whole relief, even though they had all been expecting it.

'Of course, I realize I'm not going to fill Mr Penny's shoes right away.' He was anxious for Hollis to understand from the start what a reasonable character he was. 'It's a matter of earning trust and respect.'

'Yes, skip.'

'But I hope that one day you'll all feel about me the same way you felt about Tom Penny.'

Hollis, slowing to turn into a long residential street lined with identical bow windows and tiny porches behind identical clipped hedges, glanced at him curiously. 'Well, you never know your luck.'

Corrie detected a peculiar note in Hollis's voice; but before he could follow the matter up, his attention was distracted by someone coming out of one of the front doors. The youth, carrying a holdall, clocked the police car and ducked back behind the hedge.

'Hang about!' snapped Corrie. 'We'll have him.'

Hollis was taken by surprise. 'What's happening?'

'Suspected break-in. Stop.'

Hollis braked hard. Corrie was already opening the door and leaping out before the car had stopped. Hollis was in less of a hurry. Apprehensively he said: 'Hang on, I'll call in and . . .'

Corrie reached the gate to the small patch of front garden. Before he could tackle the youth crouching below the hedge, three others launched themselves from where they had been hiding by the side gate. They were big and brawny, and grinning with menace. In the background Corrie heard Hollis wailing 'Stone the crows' and then 'Sierra Oscar, Sierra Oscar'; then the three had knocked him to the ground and were kicking him in the side. Winded, Corrie rolled over, trying to protect his head as another boot went heavily into his shoulder.

Then they had gone. As their footsteps pounded away down the road, Hollis officiously hurried towards the prone sergeant and began to help him up.

'You all right, skip?'

Corrie could not summon up the breath to reply. He leaned heavily on Hollis and tottered towards the car. He was easing himself painfully in, clutching the edge of the door, as Hollis became reproachful. 'That was a bit risky, you know, sarge. I mean, you see somebody doing a bit of dodgy work like that, you call for assistance and *then* tackle them.'

Another car came racing round the far end of the street, and Steve Loxton drew up with a jerk alongside them.

'Where's all these hordes of villains, then?'

'Halfway to Harrogate by now.' Hollis lowered his voice, but Corrie, doubled up and hugging his stomach, caught a few snatches. 'Supposed to look after our welfare . . . I mean, he put me at risk . . .'

'And that's not easily done, Reg.'

Corrie regained sufficient breath to say it was time they all got back to the station. He cursed himself as they went; and cursed again as a large chunk of front tooth fell out on to his lap. Of course that miserable coward Hollis had been right. He ought to have summoned assistance instead of going in there baldheaded like a probationer. But how was he to know there were four of them instead of just the one he had spotted?

Dismally he cleaned himself up before settling down to

prepare an official report on the incident. There was a long gash in his uniform that would have to wait, and when he got round to talking to anyone he would have to check whether there would be a whistle through the gap in his teeth.

As he was crossing front office on his way back, he saw through the glass the figure of Tom Penny stopping at the police door into the building. Penny was trying to operate the keypad in the usual way, but getting nowhere.

At the desk, Tony Stamp leaned forward and signalled towards the public entrance, operating the button so that Penny could come in the way any ordinary civilian would be allowed in.

'Code's been changed, skipper. While you were . . . away.'

'I've got an appointment with Mr Brownlow.'

'Yeah, right.' Stamp let him through to the stairs. 'How you doing?'

'I'll manage. Have to, won't I?'

Corrie wondered whether to intercept Penny and remind him of their meeting some while back, and make some friendly remark about living up to the old tradition. But quite apart from the uncertainty about speaking through his sore lips and through that grinning space between his teeth, there was something in Penny's set expression that persuaded him otherwise.

Tom Penny had stood outside the station for an interminable five minutes, nerving himself to go up to that familiar door and walk in. When he found that the keypad would not respond, it was nearly enough to make him turn round and scurry off. But now he was inside, braced to hear platitudes from Chief Superintendent Brownlow and go through the ritual of handing in his uniform.

He could have done without meeting Alec Peters and Bob Cryer on the stairs as he went up.

'Hello, Tom. Good to see you, mate.' Alec Peters had always tended to be on the cheerful side, but this was ridiculous.

'Tom.' At least Cryer had the grace to play it sober and restrained.

Penny nodded. It was all he was capable of.

'Well, all the best.' Peters was blathering on. 'I've just got to go and . . . er . . .' He waved a file as if it had suddenly become red-hot, and quickened his pace down the stairs. 'Catch you later, maybe.'

Bob Cryer said: 'We'll get together, Tom. You'll have to bring Wendy round for a meal.'

'You must come to us,' said Penny quickly.

'We'll work something out.'

They both knew this get-together was never likely to take place. But Cryer smiled, and Penny smiled and went on his way to the Chief Super's office.

He had not expected to find Chief Inspector Dewhurst and Sergeant Tanner in there along with Brownlow. They all shook hands stiffly. He had heard that in the old days the executioner, be he headsman or hangman, had invariably shaken hands with the condemned man, just to prove to him that there was no ill-feeling.

After these formalities, Dewhurst handed over a document. 'Sergeant Penny, this is formal notification that a disciplinary inquiry will be held into your criminal conviction.'

Penny nodded and accepted the document. There was not much else to do. Tearing it up and throwing it on the floor at their feet might be satisfying for a moment or two, but could have no lasting effect.

'Sit down, gentlemen.' Brownlow was at his smoothest. When they were all settled, he propped his elbows on his desk and stared earnestly at Penny. His voice was at its most calculatedly sincere. 'First of all, Tom, on a personal note I would like to begin by expressing my own profound regret at this turn of events. Whatever happens, in my view the Force

158

owes you a debt for the service, and, indeed, the sacrifice, that you've given us.'

Penny had not been in danger of crumbling until now. Whatever he had said or thought about his superiors – and he had said and thought plenty – this was just the sort of thing to get through to him and undermine all his bitter resolves. It told him what he had always wanted to hear about himself, but which nobody had ever got round to mentioning until now. Now, when it was too late.

He found it hard to speak. 'Thank you, sir.'

Dewhurst cleared his throat. 'Sergeant Penny, you are aware that you're entitled to be advised and represented by a Friend in the course of this inquiry?'

Penny grimaced at the thought of Reg Hollis fussing his way into the act.

'Yes, Tom,' Brownlow urged. 'It may well be in your own interests to consult the Federation about this, if you haven't already done so.'

'I don't think that will be necessary, sir.' Penny drew an envelope from his inside pocket and passed it across the desk. 'I'm submitting my resignation from the Force on medical grounds. My doctor will be in communication with the chief medical officer to give him the full details.'

The sense of relief in the room was so palpable that for a moment he regretted having played into their hands. Maybe it was still not too late to wipe those self-satisfied grins off their faces. He could still put up a fight, and if necessary go down fighting. But he was too tired. The weight of these few weeks of waiting had become too much.

'Well, of course I can't prejudge the outcome of the chief inspector's inquiry under these circumstances.' Brownlow looked invitingly at Dewhurst.

'Given all the relevant facts, if the chief medical officer's satisfied, I wouldn't imagine we would want to take the matter any further,' Dewhurst conceded.

Brownlow sat back, well content. 'And I can confidently

say that in that event, Tom, you would leave the Force with excellent testimonials to your character and conduct.'

The problem had been solved, the line drawn under the final total. Now all that was left was to shrug off the last remnants of his police career: the uniform, the whistle, the bits and pieces.

He stood in the Sun Hill property store while the stores liaison officer produced a large brown paper bag and began ticking off each item as it was dropped in. Tunics, two; pairs of trousers, two; boots, three pairs. Penny watched the evidence of years of his life disappearing into a paper bag.

'Of course,' said the SLO chattily, 'you're browned off right now. Can't imagine life without the job. That's the way it is, right?'

'What do you know about it?'

'Well, I see it all the time. But nobody ever *really* leaves, you know.' When Tom Penny looked blank, he went on knowledgeably: 'Once a copper, always a copper. It's a state of mind.'

Penny pushed his helmet, stick and whistle across the counter. 'Let's get this over, shall we?'

'You may not believe me, but you'll see. In the years to come you'll keep in touch. You'll know all about your old mates: who's been transferred, who's got promotion. You'll sit at home, looking at the clock and guessing where they all are at that time. Thinking about them all getting on with the job.'

It sounded like being sentenced all over again, this time to an eternal purgatory. Penny waited with mounting nausea for the final items to be ticked off, but the SLO was in confiding mood, larkily prodding at the collection on his counter. 'Y'know, in my experience blokes invariably lose their helmet, stick and whistle.'

'Well, I haven't.'

'Souvenirs, if you know what I mean.' The SLO was doing

160

his best with this dim customer. 'Mementoes of your police service.'

Penny picked up the stick and whistle, dropped them in the upturned helmet, and handed the lot over.

'Stuff them,' he said. At the door he looked back. 'And make it easy on yourself. Start with the whistle and work upwards.'

Chief Inspector Conway and Inspector Monroe stood at Conway's window and watched Tom Penny cross the street below. He stopped for a few seconds on the opposite pavement as if his feet refused to go on carrying him away from Sun Hill once and for all.

'Tragic, really,' Conway muttered.

'A lesson to us all, sir.'

'Hm.' Conway waited until Penny had turned the corner and was out of sight. He hoped he was not making for that pub where the trouble had started. Or any other pub, for that matter. 'Still, the job goes on.' He fired the question without preamble: 'How would you feel about Corrie as a permanent replacement?'

Monroe barely hesitated. 'Frankly I don't think he commands the requisite respect. And that business this morning gives me grave doubts about his judgement out on the ground.'

'I take your point.'

'Perhaps we should be looking for a younger man. Someone keen to bring himself to notice, more willing to exert authority.'

Conway nodded. It was all too true that 'A' Relief was well supplied with maturity and experience at the sergeant level. A bit of energy and innovation might enrich the mixture.

'Stir them up a bit.' Monroe echoed his thoughts.

'I'm glad we're thinking along the same lines, Andrew.'

It was a pity about Tom Penny. But, thought Conway, it's an ill wind . . .

161

Thirteen

June Ackland turned over in bed and groped for the edge of the duvet before it could slide off to the floor. She was in the process of sleepily hauling it back when she became aware of daylight round the edge of the curtains. It ought not to be daylight yet. There ought still to be the bronze glow of the street lamp on the corner. She rolled over and blinked at the digits on her bedside clock. It was a quarter to six. She must have slept through the alarm.

Tumbling out of bed, she spluttered angrily to herself as she headed for the bathroom. If she hadn't stayed up so late, waiting for that lousy man who never showed . . . if she hadn't started on the bottle of wine she had been keeping for the two of them, and finished it just to calm her misery, and then sunk into her chair before that dismal television programme she couldn't summon up the energy to switch off . . .

If she had never met Gordon Wray, or at least never let herself drift into this hopeless affair . . .

There was no time for breakfast. She went out breathless into the street and along to the main road, and spent a desperate five minutes crossing and re-crossing it in the hope of seeing a taxi's blob of light. It was never an area for any busy trade in taxis, and least of all at this hour of the morning. She debated whether or not to risk waving at the driver of a pickup truck rattling out of a scrapyard, but took one look at his face and decided against it. At last a taxi came in sight, far away. She waved frantically, begging it not to turn down a side street and head back west. She could have whimpered with joy as it came on and slewed in to the kerb.

'Sun Hill police station.'

'Done something wrong, love?'

She looked apprehensively at her watch. 'As a matter of fact, I have.'

She was aware of the driver glancing curiously at her in his mirror as they overtook a bus and turned into a maze of back doubles. She thankfully discovered that the man knew his stuff: this twisting and turning route would get her there a lot more quickly than the more obvious shopping streets with their sequences of traffic lights turning to red even when there was no vehicle in sight.

Parade had been over a good three quarters of an hour when she arrived, and the relief was out on the streets. Sergeant Peters, not in his usual amiable mood, raised an unwelcoming eyebrow as she bustled in.

'Sarge, I'm sorry. I've never . . . I don't know what . . .'

'Neither do I, I'm sure. Not like you, Ackland.'

She guessed that this was definitely going to be an Ackland day, not a June one.

'I'm sorry,' she said again. 'Truly I am, sarge. I don't know why my alarm didn't go off. Or whether it did or didn't, anyway. And I didn't stop to check.'

'Better go and get into uniform. And you can spend the first shift in the CAD room. Take over from Delia. I want to run over a few things with her, and then she'll be picking up some gen from the collator.'

June went sheepishly away.

It was a quiet morning. Stringer rang in with a couple of queries about iffy vehicles, and she made a note to hand on the details to Ron Smollett when he arrived. There was usually a blank spell when nobody rang in to complain or set off indignant alarms, unless there had been an overnight break-in or somebody had been beaten up and dumped in a back alley. It might have been better if things had been busy. It would have given her less time to brood on what was happening in her life; or threatening not to happen.

Dave Quinnan's voice came on the line. He wanted to know if there had been any requests to keep an eye on a damaged shop front at the end of the mall, but when he recognized Ackland's voice he brightened. 'Missed you this morning, June.'

'So did everybody.'

'Fancy you being in CAD. Thought you were still under the CID.'

'Look here, Quinnan – '

But Quinnan had cheerfully signed off.

A few minutes after nine o'clock she received a summons via Sergeant Peters to go and see Inspector Monroe. Alec Peters looked more human now, on the verge of offering some encouraging remark. Instead, he saw Datta coming in off patrol and waved to her to take Ackland's place for five or ten minutes, or however long Monroe chose to make the interview.

Ackland went dismally to the duty inspector's office. She was sure she had not been sent for in order to be commended, or for any casual routine query.

'You wanted to see me, sir.'

Monroe looked up from a sheaf of papers, and waved her towards a chair. He looked uncomfortable, yet unexpectedly friendly. Only maybe the friendliness was a mix of uncertainty and embarrassment.

'Ah, yes, June.'

She had not expected to be called June. Instead of putting her at her ease, it worried her. She had spent a dismal couple of hours since getting here. There was no use shuffling round the issue. She decided to tackle it head on and be done with it. 'Look, sir, if it's about this morning, I'm sorry. I've already told the skipper. There's no excuse.'

He looked even less at ease, utterly unlike his usual brusque and bossy self. 'I'm not going to make a song and dance about it, June. By the way, would you like a cup of tea? Coffee?'

These civilities were getting even more worrying. 'No, no thanks.'

'Sure? Well, about this morning. While lateness is never to be condoned, I know it's quite out of character in an officer of your experience and professionalism.' He fiddled with a pen. 'And that makes me wonder if . . . well . . . if there might be any problems of a personal nature. Putting you off your stroke a bit, sort of thing.'

So that was it. She braced herself. 'Just because I overslept, just once?'

'No, no. But, well' – Monroe would obviously rather have been anywhere else but here – 'I do have to keep my ear to the ground or I wouldn't be doing my job.'

'Canteen gossip?' she stonewalled.

'More than just gossip, June. All I'm asking is, are there any matters troubling you that you feel you want to tell me about?'

'No.'

He sighed. 'Well, that's it, then. If you change your mind, the door's always open.'

'Thank you, sir.'

She restrained herself from saying that he could leave his door open as long as he liked, and all he would get would be a draught.

She turned the corner of the corridor on her way back to the CAD room, and found herself face to face with Gordon Wray.

He glanced over his shoulder and said quickly, in an undertone: 'June – '

'Hi.' She tried to go on her way, but he pushed his right hand against the wall and stopped her.

'Look, June, I'm sorry about last night. I couldn't get away.'

'Doesn't matter.'

165

'And I couldn't risk phoning. Angela was around all evening.'

His pale eyes, which could be so hypnotic and persuasive, glanced watchfully past her. He was probably as twitchy and apprehensive as this at home. Not much fun, really. All at once she felt quite detached, quite sorry for him. 'It's all right. I guessed something must have happened. Don't worry about it.'

'It would have looked really odd if I'd made a call and not told her who it was.'

'Relax, Gordon.' Crazily she felt much wiser and more mature than he was. 'I do know this game. It's par for the course. Big girls don't cry.'

'We'll fix something up.'

'Sure.'

It was pitiful to see how relieved he was. And in no time at all he would be congratulating himself on having such an understanding mistress.

As she passed the open door of the collator's room she heard Ron Smollett laying it on all heavy and pretentious with Delia French.

'Like I say, Delia, if you have any problems, don't be afraid to ask. There aren't many angles I can't get my head round.'

That was true, thought Ackland wryly. Ron Smollett had talked himself out of many a scrape and into many a sly little deal during his years in the Force. He knew how to get hold of everything from a quick respray on a scratched Panda to tickets for the Centre Court at Wimbledon. After twenty years in Traffic Division he had landed the Local Intelligence Officer's job as the result of the last of many crashes, but that was not going to cramp his style. He knew every detail of administrative routine; and also knew all the tricks in the trade. And he liked other people to be aware of this.

'Now,' he pontificated, 'starting with your Form 78, that records the juvenile offence. And then, depending on what action's going to be taken – '

166

'You want a Form 70 if he's appearing in court,' Delia interrupted, 'or a Form 74 if it's a final caution. But anyway this is down to Youth and Community Section. We wouldn't be handling it here.'

'Er, no.' Smollett bristled. He was not a man who enjoyed being corrected or crossed. 'But I'm telling you about it because you can never know too much about how the system works.'

In spite of her depression, June Ackland could not help grinning to herself. Delia French knew all about every last little detail of that kind from the days when she had supervised the typing pool. When it came to forms and procedures there was not much Ron Smollett could teach her; and he might regret trying.

'Of course,' Smollett went on in a more conciliatory mood, 'there might be some questions that come up that can't be fully explored within the confines of the nick. I wouldn't begrudge spending a bit of extra time, informally, so to speak. Perhaps after a drink.'

June Ackland moaned silently to herself. Another one of them getting randy in the middle of the morning. But there must be a bright side to this. Whatever Smollett had in his grubby little mind, she thought he would get quite a shock tackling Delia.

The whole thing was such a sour joke, really. Only it was sometimes difficult to laugh it off.

DCI Wray settled himself at his desk. It had been sticky, those few moments. He had not been looking forward to encountering June this morning and having to make those excuses, even though they were true. But he could congratulate himself that it had all gone off very smoothly. He was in a relaxed, amenable mood when Sergeant Greig tapped on the door and came in with a bulging file.

'You got five minutes, guv?'

'Sure, Alastair. Pull up a chair.'

'It's about this fraud.' Greig, as usual, sounded very earnest. To him every case was the biggest thing since the Great Train Robbery. 'Mr Khan and Daisy Daydream Dresses. I thought I'd run it past you, because the whole picture's a bit complicated, and I want to make sure we're moving on the right lines.'

In more tetchy mood Wray might have accused him of shielding his own back by trying to shoulder someone else with responsibility. As it was, he simply felt a tolerant amusement, and leaned back in his chair. 'Kiting cheques, isn't he?'

'Well, that's only part of it.'

'We'll get it sorted out. It's about time we had a chat, anyway, Alastair.'

'Guv?' One of Greig's worst failings was an inability to switch from one subject to another at a moment's notice. Once he had got his teeth into something, he preferred to worry away at it to the exclusion of everything else.

'Got to keep close to the troops,' said Wray expansively. 'That's what goes wrong with police management: we lose sight of what's going on down at the sharp end.'

'Yes, I suppose that's always a danger.' Greig looked wistfully at his file, and made an effort to drag his attention away from it.

'I mean,' said Wray, 'I've been trying to change the way we operate in CID. But without feedback from forward-looking officers like yourself, I'm often working in the dark. So let's be hearing from you. How do you feel about the way things have been going round here lately? It goes without saying that you can speak freely.'

Now Greig seemed quite happy to abandon his fraud file for the time being. He thought for a few moments, then said: 'In my view we're moving in a very positive direction. And what's really remarkable is that we've come so far, so quickly.'

This was exactly what Wray wanted to hear, even making allowances for a certain amount of flannel on Greig's part. He said: 'If I'd told you, when I first came here, that in due course we'd have Frank Burnside coming along to meetings with detailed budgets for his operations, what would you have thought?'

'I'd never have believed it.'

'And Ted Roach beavering away on the Beat Crime Liaison Committee!'

It was true, of course, that Roach hated the sight of every fellow member of that committee, but the thing was that he wasn't doing at all a bad job. Wray felt he could be proud of what he had achieved so far, and was not averse to accepting a little flattery from Alastair Greig. In the CID offices there was a lot of big talk as if their snouts and their street cred were all that mattered, but in fact he was gradually getting them to pay attention to the paperwork these days. It was quite an achievement. And after all, it was the paperwork that made a good result stand up in court.

Greig said: 'If you don't mind me asking, guv, how do you see *your* career developing after Sun Hill?'

Greig was no fool. Wray knew that this was blatant buttering-up, but he did not disapprove. That was how you got on in this job. 'I've made some useful contacts at Area,' he said. 'I think the Major Incident Team's a logical step up. And if I do go that route – well, I have every intention of bringing on right-thinking officers. You can depend on that, Alastair.'

This was clearly what Detective Sergeant Greig wanted to hear. Wray was fairly certain now that he had established Greig as a loyal ally. With resentful folk like Frank Burnside around, still feeling that he ought to have won promotion to DCI, it was a good thing to ensure a bit of loyalty somewhere, in case of need.

His phone rang. It was Marion, Brownlow's secretary, asking him to come to the Chief Super's office at once. Wray was puzzled. He had already arranged a routine meeting with the Chief Super later in the day. But if he was summoned, then he was summoned. Never lose a chance of impressing the big boss.

He put the phone down and got up. 'Got to go see the Old Man.'

Greig's attention was drifting back to his file. 'We never actually got round to the fraud.'

'Tell you what, Alastair. If it's complicated, lay it on a flow chart. Use different coloured inks. Always makes a good impression.'

He winked, Greig smiled conspiratorially, and Wray went along to Brownlow's office in a high good humour. Things were really working out very well, one way and another.

The Chief Super indicated the chair facing the desk, and waited until Wray was settled before launching his thunderbolt.

'I won't beat about the bush, Gordon, because there's no way of wrapping this one up. You're being transferred.'

Wray felt it like a kick in the stomach. He could hardly find the breath for a reply. And what sort of reply was there, anyway, to such an incredible statement?

'Effective from next Monday,' Brownlow went on grimly. 'Your new post will be that of Chief Instructor, CID Training School.'

'Will it hell!'

'You're not being asked to vote on it, Gordon. You're being told a fact.' Brownlow slowed down, now that the first assault had been slammed home. 'Look, I know this comes at you out of the blue – '

'This comes straight off the wall,' Wray blurted out. It was unbelievable. He had come to this station at Brownlow's own invitation, had knocked a bunch of cowboys into something resembling a Criminal Investigation Department, only to have this flung at him. 'I'm just getting things to rights here, and now I'm being kicked into touch. I don't get it.'

'Nobody's denying your contribution to the effectiveness and efficiency of this Division.' Brownlow was making it even slower and more ponderous. 'Sadly that's not the only consideration.'

170

Now Wray began to get the measure of what had hit him. But it was an outrage. Incredible. He forced himself to slow down to Brownlow's pace, and play the innocent. 'What am I to make of that, sir?'

'Never mind the games, Gordon. You know perfectly well what I'm talking about.' Brownlow waited, but Wray had no intention of yielding him even an inch. He folded his arms. Let Brownlow spell it out. His brow darkening, Brownlow did just that: 'You've been having an affair with a WPC. You can hardly imagine that something like that stays a secret.'

'With all due respect, sir, I don't intend to discuss my private life with you. I'd like to know what disciplinary offence I've committed.'

'You haven't committed a disciplinary offence.'

'Then why am I being punished?'

'You're being transferred, not punished.'

'Don't insult my intelligence, sir.'

'I would have thought someone with your commitment to training and innovation would see great opportunities in being an instructor.' Brownlow was now trying a mild, emollient tack.

Wray was having none of it. 'That's not the point. It takes me out of line operationally, which means I'm off the promotion ladder.'

'This whole business is a matter of great regret to me, Gordon, but it's been settled from above. There's nothing I can do about it.'

'If you think I'm just going to roll over for this, you're making one hell of a mistake.'

'Perhaps we can have another talk about this later, when you're in control of your temper.'

Wray shoved his chair back and marched to the door. As he opened it he turned back for just one question. 'Is it too late to take up your kind offer a while back, and learn the funny handshake?'

Brownlow said icily: 'I'll do you the courtesy of ignoring that remark.'

Wray suppressed a retort that he didn't want the remark ignored. He wanted it kept out in the open until somebody had the guts to answer it. But he carried the thought, seething within him, back to CID office. Greig was rummaging in the stationery cupboard, presumably trying to find some felt-tipped pens for the colouring job Wray had suggested. Frank Burnside looked up as the DCI crossed the outer office, preparing to say something. Wray gave him no chance, but went into his own office and slammed the door. Let them make what they liked of it.

He was sweating with rage. He took off his jacket and loosened his tie. There had to be something to say, but who could he say it to? Certainly not Burnside, Greig, or any of the rest of them. Everything had been so rosy such a short time before, talking to Greig. Now there would be no more talking. They would all hear soon enough, they'd be quick enough to dodge him during his last days here. He could almost hear Burnside's vengeful snigger. Not that Burnside stood any chance of stepping into his shoes.

There was someone who had to know. He reached for his phone and asked if WPC Ackland could come to his office, making it as brisk and impersonal as possible. Alec Peters, who took the message, sounded cool and equally impersonal.

June was a lot less so as she came into his room. 'I hope this is business, Gordon. Because it's a bit embarrassing, being sent for. There's some of them . . .' Her voice trailed away as she saw that something was wrong. 'What's the matter?'

'Brownlow's the matter. He's trying to give me the elbow.'

She looked lost and puzzled. He had had to speak to her, yet now she was here he found himself almost wondering who she was and how she could have caused such damage to his career.

'What d'you mean?' The sound of her voice had been one of the things that had most attracted him. Especially in the

172

darkness, at certain times. Now it had become thin and mean-ingless.

'Just told me I'm being transferred,' he flung at her. 'Side-lined into CID Training School. Which would mean I've done my legs as far as promotion's concerned.'

She stared. She put out a hand to him, then let it fall limply to her side. 'Because of me?' When he nodded, she shook her head, stunned. 'They can't do that.'

'You know the job. They think they can do what they bloody like.'

'But it's so *stupid*.'

His first fury was falling back like a wave that had lost its force, trickling away with a forlorn murmur over the shore. 'The brass can tolerate these things as long as there's no fuss. But for some reason it's become an embarrassment. Don't know why, but I do know it's the sort of thing they can't cope with.'

'Well, they don't have to cope with it. What's the point of blowing it up now, when it's . . . well, when it's practically over. Isn't it?'

Looking at her pert yet vulnerable face, and those lips that always looked slightly bruised, all at once he wanted it not to be over; wanted to go back to the beginning and play it better this time, avoid the pitfalls this time. But it was too late. She was telling the truth which he would not have had the guts to put into words.

'Don't look at me like that, Gordon,' she went on quietly. 'You know it's true. How often have we seen each other in the last few weeks?'

'It's been difficult,' he said dismally.

'It's been difficult because you're not prepared to be a bas-tard to your wife and kids. I'm not asking you to be. There's no future in it.'

He leaned forward despondently on his desk. 'I never meant to mess you about, June.'

'Oh, it's all right.' She laughed a mirthless laugh. 'When

173

you've had your candy floss, all you're left with is the stick. I found that out years ago. The point is, they're creating more problems by splitting us up than by letting things be.'

'But they don't understand that.'

'Well, tell Brownlow it's all over. You've got to fight it, Gordon. It's your career on the line.'

He forced a wry smile. Trying to make this outfit admit there had been a mistake and that a few second thoughts wouldn't come amiss was a pretty tall order. All the same, he would like to give them a run for their money.

'But what I need to know,' he said bleakly, 'is who grassed on us.'

'Oh, come on, now. Everybody knew, more or less.'

'Yes, but some interfering prat's gone out of his way to make an issue of it. Somebody holier-than-thou, somewhere in this building.'

June blinked and let out a little, despairing groan as if things were only just fitting into place. 'Monroe,' she breathed.

'Monroe? Why him in particular?'

June Ackland's bruised, vulnerable look was changing to one of cold rage, as if she had just stumbled on some treachery that ought to have been obvious from the start. 'He's got a thing about affairs between officers,' she said bitterly. 'He tried to give me the old Dutch uncle routine only this morning. It was like watching a gorilla doing brain surgery.'

'But would he grass on you – make such a big thing out of it?'

'Who else?' She was on her way to the door. 'I'm going to see him about it. We'll have this out in the open.'

Wray had thought there would be no more shocks left this morning. But the thought of her marching in on Monroe and blowing her top was a frightening one. 'Don't dig yourself in it, June.'

'I'm already in it,' she said fiercely. 'Monroe's my guv'nor. He's got no right to pull a filthy stroke like this.'

174

That cold light in her eyes made her more alive than he had ever seen her. And sexier. For all the good that was, now.

She marched vengefully out.

Fourteen

Alastair Greig had cleared the top of his desk and laid out a sheet of flipchart paper. After some rummaging in the cupboard he had at last found a set of coloured felt-tip pens and began laying them methodically in a line above the paper. When one of them rolled a few millimetres out of true, he tapped it back into place and studied the pattern with some satisfaction.

Burnside had been watching with steadily mounting disbelief. When he could restrain himself no longer he said: 'What about the plasticine, while you're at it? I always thought this was supposed to be a CID office, not a pre-school playgroup.'

'I am trying,' said Greig loftily, 'to find a clear and helpful way to present some problematic information.'

'Ask Viv. She might lend you a needle and cotton. You can embroider it on your sporran.'

Before Greig could muster a suitable retort, June Ackland stormed past the window of the office, on her way from Wray's room. It did not look as if they had had much in the way of a loving get-together.

'Just what's all that door slamming and stomping about add up to?' Burnside raised an eyebrow at Greig. 'Alastair, don't tell me you forgot to warm the bog seat for him this morning?'

Greig ignored this and set to work contriving a complex of arrows, triangles and boxes in different colours. Viv Martella leaned over his shoulder, more respectful than the DI.

'How does that show the laundered cheques, then?'

'That'll be in red. I've only done the green and blue bits so far.'

She watched him painstakingly link a sequence of boxes, and slowly shook her head. After a moment she stabbed at one of the lines with a crimson fingernail. There were quite a lot of colours in play now as she indicated that in one congested spot he had got cheques going into the junction in green ink and coming out way down the line in blue. Hating to be interrupted, Greig started to explain that the cheques to one side were from building society accounts, not from customers. Halfway through the lecture he stopped, looked again, and then tore the sheet off and crumpled it up. After all, it had only been a first draft.

Martella went off to the collator's room to return a load of files to Ron Smollett.

'And don't interrupt his training session with Delia,' Burnside called after her, 'unless Delia's got him on the floor in an armlock.'

Greig tried to concentrate on the intricate job before him. On his second attempt he was confident he was on the way to getting it right. It would really be very useful when analysing the whole Daisy Daydream set-up and deciding which way to pounce. Wray ought to be pleased with him. That was another thing about which he was feeling increasingly confident: that Detective Chief Inspector Wray was on the way up and had every intention of rewarding a conscientious member of his team.

It came as a nasty blow when Viv Martella returned, in a greater hurry than she had left, and broke the news with a dramatic flourish.

'He's out.' She nodded towards DCI Wray's inner door.

'What d'you mean, out?' Burnside snorted. 'Hasn't sneaked past us so far as I know.'

'On his ear. Off to Detective Training School, effective next Monday.'

'Is this kosher?'

'According to Smollett.'

'Who'd be the first to know, as usual.' Burnside winced in grudging sympathy. 'Poor old Gordon. What a choker.' A malevolent grin tugged at his lips. 'Bit gutty for you, Alastair, after all that time you put in on your knees.'

Greig looked unhappily at his web of lines and coloured blobs. 'Actually, I must say I think it's very bad news for this nick.'

'You do, eh?'

'Oh, well.' Greig looked briefly up at Burnside. 'Back to the Stone Age, eh, guv?'

Burnside's grin stayed fixed as he waited to see if there was any more sardonic stuff to come. When he was sure that Alastair Greig had decided that immersing himself again in his work was the better part of valour, he went off to find Bob Cryer, or Alec Peters, or anyone who might know exactly how things were working out and why. There might even be someone who hadn't heard yet, and then he would have the pleasure of imparting the gossip himself.

One person he would not contact for the time being was Gordon Wray.

The news had already reached the canteen. Leaving with Stamp to go back on foot patrol, Reg Hollis said eagerly: 'You heard the latest?'

'Go on, Reg. Indulge yourself.'

'DCI's got binned.'

'What, for going OTS?'

Hollis nodded gleefully. 'Done his legs.'

Stamp whistled reflectively. 'Hope for his sake it was worth it.'

They walked for a while in silence along the High Street, brooding on human mortality and survival both spiritual and physical.

As they passed a butcher's shop Hollis said: 'Could you function without meat, d'you reckon?'

178

'Dunno about function. Survive, I suppose.'

'Do you remember Linda, that WPC in the Youth and Community Section?'

'Not half.' Stamp sighed reminiscently.

'She gave up on the canteen entirely when she became a vegetarian. They couldn't accommodate her.'

'Linda was vegetarian?'

'Couldn't bring herself to touch meat.'

'Must have thought I was a pickled cucumber,' murmured Stamp.

Hollis was paying little attention, immersed in contemplation of his own moral and digestive problems. 'I can't help thinking, if I didn't eat meat, I'm sure I'd lose my vigour.'

'Oh, it's down to meat, is it?'

The butcher's shop-front well behind them, they were approaching a sandwich takeaway. Two teenage lads suddenly erupted from the doorway, waving bottles of some pink mineral water. 'That so?' one of them was yelling. 'Well, stuff your poxy shop.' The other raised his bottle above his head and hurled it at the window. There was a splintering of glass. 'Scumbag!'

Stamp broke into a run. Hollis followed, a few paces behind. The smaller of the two lads bolted down an alley, and Hollis chose him as the lesser of two dangers. They were only a few feet apart when the youth vaulted over a low wall and made off into the tangle of a high rise estate. Hollis found himself facing a fine choice of stairways and alleys between buildings. There was obviously no point in continuing. He took off his helmet, mopped his brow, and abandoned the pursuit.

Stamp had followed the other rowdy through a gap in the traffic but was losing ground when his quarry cannoned into a passer-by and stumbled. Stamp put on a last wild spurt and had him collared, and called in: 'Sierra Oscar from 596, receiving . . .'

As he delivered his catch to Sun Hill, he found himself remembering the shapely Linda and regretting that she was no longer around. But if she had still been here, would he have been in the same kind of trouble as Wray now seemed to be in? He doubted it.

Maybe, with Wray out of the way, it might be worth while having another attempt on June Ackland. Thoughts on those lines kept his imagination happily occupied for the rest of the morning.

Inspector Monroe had obviously not been expecting to see June Ackland again quite so soon. He looked up from his desk and tried to smile non-committally, not being sure what to prepare for.

She said: 'You did tell me your door was always open, sir.'

'Yes, of course, June.'

'I decided I would like a discussion of a purely personal nature, after all.' She had come here determined to keep her anger finely tuned, and not to blunder too noisily all over the place. 'Strictly between these walls.'

'Man to man, eh?'

His attempted bonhomie sickened her. She closed the door sharply behind her. 'Let's see if either of us qualifies, shall we?'

Without waiting to be invited she pulled a chair up to the desk and sat down. From here she could let him have it right between the eyes; and that was where he was going to get it. Still she meant to keep her voice down, though once she really got going she heard herself saying things that had been bottled up for a long time and were not what she had originally meant to kick off with. Somehow it was becoming essential to spill the whole lot, get it all off her chest at one go.

'Since you took over this relief,' she said with lethal deliberation, 'you've established yourself as a petty-minded, rule-bound little Hitler with all the warmth and humour of a rusted Dalek.' His mouth opened, but no words came out. With a contemptuous shrug she went on: 'That's fair enough, we can live with that if we have to. But there's a bottom line in this

180

job, and that's loyalty – ours to you, and you to us. All right, we can step out of line, you can give us grief and we'll swallow it and try and do better. But what you *don't* do' – it was no good, her voice was rising and she wanted to shout it at him and the whole flaming world – 'is grass on us, because that way you'll end up giving all the orders and nobody will be listening.'

At last he made an effort to stem the harangue. 'I think there's some misunderstanding here.'

'Oh, no. No, there's no misunderstanding. Earlier on you tried to stick your nose into my affairs and I wasn't having any. Next thing I hear, Gordon Wray's career's blown out of the water.'

Monroe stared. 'Since when? This is the first I've heard of it.'

Maybe he was telling the truth about just that one aspect. Confirmation of the pay-off of his undercover dealings hadn't reached him yet. But that made no difference. 'Well, congratulations,' she hurled at him. 'You must be really pleased with yourself. It's not often a relief inspector gets the chance to knock a high-flying DCI off his perch. Carve a notch in your truncheon.'

She paused not because she was finished but because she needed to gulp in breath.

It was Monroe's chance to bawl her out for insolence or insubordination, or whatever he chose to call it. Instead, he said: 'June, this was none of my doing. I quite understand that you're in an emotional state about this – '

'Emotional state! What do you put this down to – PMT?'

'Let me finish, please. I'll tell you what those questions of mine this morning were all about. You know Bob Eady?'

For a moment the name meant nothing; then she remembered the interview training course she had been on with fellow officers from Sun Hill a few months back. She nodded, remembering her impression that she had made rather a good

181

showing during the simulated interviews and the challenges that had been thrown up. It came as a shock to learn different.

'He happens to be an old mate of mine,' Monroe was continuing. 'He told me about remarks he picked up during that course you were on – and some hints in the pub afterwards – suggesting you were under a lot of pressure as a result of this relationship with the DCI. He didn't put in any official reference to this, but he did tell me. I felt it was my duty to say something to you. I didn't enjoy it, and I obviously made a pills of it. But you're a great asset to this relief, and I couldn't just stand by without asking if you needed help.'

It sounded so plausible. But that was Monroe all over: bossy half the time, sly the rest of it.

She said: 'So then you had to dash off and blow it up to Brownlow.'

'No, I didn't.'

'I don't believe you.'

'What more can I say?'

He looked stricken, as if wondering how to cope if this was the way everybody else regarded him. June Ackland was glad about that, anyway. Let him wriggle. She stood up, ready to deliver her final blast. If it meant the end of her career as well as Gordon Wray's, that was just too bad. There came a time when all the pent-up words had to be allowed to pour out, and this was well and truly the time. 'Like I said, you've done a lot to make yourself unpopular on this relief. But you did have some respect. We never took you for a liar.'

This time she closed the door very quietly.

The door of DCI Wray's office opened. He had been sitting with his chair swivelled towards the window, numb and unseeing. When he looked round, ready to snarl at any interruption, he found Derek Conway, in civvies, waiting in the doorway to gauge his likely reception before entering.

'We should have a chat, Gordon?'

So somebody from Uniform couldn't help coming to gloat.

Wray supposed there would be a whole string of them in due course. Waiting for him to cry on their shoulder, or buy them a beer, or warn them against falling into the same errors he had been trapped in. He was tempted to wave Conway out of the room. But the two of them had always been on tolerably good terms. Conway, whatever his faults of doggedness, lack of humour and lack of any really sparkling talent, was straight in his dealings and had backed CID up more than once in post-mortem niggles with the top brass.

Wray got up from his chair and reached wearily for his jacket. 'Obviously the glad tidings have reached you.'

Conway glanced back along the corridor. Equally obviously he did not want other people to know about him being here. That was an aspect which Wray had not so far considered. Maybe, instead of hurrying to gloat over him, they would all find ways of steering clear. He was a leper. It could be bad luck to associate with someone so definitively on the way out.

'Middle of the yarder – makes sense, eh?'

Which confirmed Wray's cynical view of the situation.

In fact, once they were in the station yard, Conway realized that they were overlooked by a large number of windows, and there was the chance of cars swinging in at unpredictable times. He quickened his pace and led them out into the street, round the corner and along a secluded terrace of two-storey Edwardian houses which had seen better days.

Further confirmation came with his first remark since leaving the station.

'This conversation isn't taking place, right?'

'Sure.'

'I mean, it's strictly between ourselves. I don't want you telling Ackland about it. Okay?'

'All right.'

Wray looked at the sequence of looped lace curtains they were passing. Such a drab, unimaginative duplication. A drab, unadventurous street, where nothing ever happened. Whether it was the nearness of Sun Hill nick or simply the

183

dullness of life here that caused it, there had never been any violent or even mild disturbance recorded in Sun Hill about this terrace. Perhaps being unadventurous could be a happy state. He would have a chance of sampling that in the months to come; and in the years to come.

'Now this thing's happened,' said Conway, 'we'd all like to see it tidied away with as little damage as possible. Are you with me?'

Wray was several steps ahead of him, in his mind if not here in the street. Of course that was what Conway and Brownlow wanted: tidying it all away with the minimum of after-effects. He began to realize just how Tom Penny had felt, such a short time ago. It was like every bad story in the tabloid papers. Once the police decided to beat you up, there was no holding them back. Only this time it was a matter of internal injuries, with nobody around to protect you.

When he made no reply, Conway went on: 'Look, everybody at Sun Hill knew you were going over the side with Ackland. But we all turned a blind eye as long as you didn't do it in the street and frighten the horses.'

'Until Monroe heard heavenly voices telling him to stamp out sin.'

'No,' said Conway fiercely, 'it wasn't Monroe.'

Wray thought of June's intensity, her absolute conviction about the source of the trouble. Knowing her, he knew she wouldn't lie, least of all on a matter like this.

'That's the way I heard it.'

'I'm telling you, Gordon, you weren't blown out from inside the nick.'

Another likely story. But of course they would have to maintain it. After all, Conway and Brownlow would have to be able to look each other in the eye the next time they rolled up their trouser legs together.

'All right,' he said sceptically. 'What's the agreed story of what happened?'

They had reached the end of the terrace and turned back,

184

side by side, like two constables on the beat. They were automatically in step.

Conway said: 'Your old lady was the Social Services representative on a panel debating care and resettlement of young offenders, right?'

'Angela?' He felt a chill of unease. 'Yes, but what's that got to do with it?'

'The police spokesman was our new Deputy Assistant Commissioner. Fresh from the turnip fields, wants to give us all a short back and sides. Well, it seems your missus had a word with him about the state of affairs at Sun Hill. And I do mean affairs.'

'But Angela doesn't know – '

'Your wife would appear to know a lot more than you think, mate.'

Wray moistened his lips. He thought he had had all the bad news he could take, but it seemed that there was more in store.

'So this morning' – Conway was not exactly enjoying himself, but he was not in a mood to pull any punches – 'our Mr Brownlow gets a phone call, passing on the DAC's surprise that our Mr Brownlow was unaware of the hanky-panky going on in his division. And telling him about your transfer. Not discussing it, or recommending it, Gordon: *telling* him. It was never in Brownlow's hands. And there's nothing he can do to square it up.'

'But why didn't he tell me this?'

'You didn't give him much of a chance, by all accounts. And besides that, I don't suppose he's all that keen on letting his underlings know that he's been getting grief from above.'

They walked for a while in silence, turning down an alley towards the canal bank. Wray turned over the unpalatable facts in his mind. Even if he made a point that the affair was over, it would be too late. The damage was done. It had got out into the open. He had done the one thing which, as a police officer of considerable experience, he should have

185

known could never be forgiven in the real, rough world: he had got caught.

He was conscious of a prickle of guilt about June. She was going to come out of this wretchedly. 'All right, so I carry the can. But when it comes to June – '

'That's what I'm on about. Explaining and complaining will just stop it being forgotten. That's why I'm saying don't tell Ackland. You know what she's like. If she thinks the DAC has been responsible, she's quite capable of picketing his office, demonstrating about justice and that sort of thing.'

It was impossible not to smile, sadly, at the thought. Of course it was true. That was June, all right.

'And that's the last thing we want,' said Conway. 'Take my advice, Gordon. And while you're at it, take your punishment. But keep your head down. Give it a year or two, you could be back on the inside track.'

It had to be accepted. That was the way it was. Conway meant well. But at the same time it was his rigid code of unimaginative routine responses to any given situation that made his good intentions little more than leaning on a lid to stop a pot boiling over. One day something like that might blow up in his face, or at least scald him a bit round the edges.

No, probably not. Not Conway.

Wray surrendered. 'All right, I get the message. I appreciate what you're saying, Derek.' But he could not resist one final dig. 'All the same, I still think I might have survived at Sun Hill if I'd been trained to be more cautious.'

'You mean staying away from the skirt?'

'I mean wiping the aprons more reverently.'

'You can believe what you like about the Masons, Gordon,' said Conway tautly. 'But with this DAC in the saddle, you could be on handshaking terms with Almighty God and it wouldn't do you any good.'

They had come full circle round the rear of Sun Hill police station, coming under the railway arch and down the slope to the sprawl of buildings. By tacit consent Derek Conway went up the main steps while Gordon Wray went through the yard to the side entrance. There were a few routine matters to be sorted out. Tomorrow there would undoubtedly have to be a final session with Brownlow, saying nothing that had not already been said but politely tying up the loose ends: making it all nice and tidy, just as Derek Conway had advocated.

Within a short time he would have to confront Angela and ask her what the hell she had been playing at. Or else let her make the running: play it cool and uncommunicative, letting her carry the knowledge that she had done them both out of the perks and profits of his promotion.

He had lost track of time. When he drove out of the yard it came as a surprise to see June Ackland coming off the relief and walking downhill from the station, dressed in the blouse and skirt and light fawn raincoat she had worn when they went off for that weekend in Salisbury. He had been so ravenously anxious to get her down there and into that hotel bedroom. Now she looked forlorn, unexciting; and pitiful. If he had not already known her and known what she was like out of those clothes, he would not have given her a second glance.

He swung in to the kerb and leaned over to wind down the window. 'I'll give you a lift.' When she glanced back instinctively at the nick, he said: 'It's a bit late to be worried one way or the other.'

'I suppose it is.' She slid into the passenger seat beside him. As he drove away she said: 'Have you been back to Brownlow?'

'We've been sorting out the nuts and bolts of my leaving office. A few more scraps tomorrow, no doubt.'

'You'll tell him it's all over between us? So there's no need for your transfer?'

'That's not on the agenda, June.'

He was staring straight ahead at the road, pretending to be alert for the notoriously haphazard local traffic and the wild

187

local kids. Beside him he sensed her brewing up to boiling point.

'If you're not going to tell him,' she said, 'then I will.'

'No, you won't. You'll drop it.' He still stared stonily ahead. 'Please. For my sake and yours. There's no point in you sticking your head in the frame for this one. It's not you they're gunning for.'

'But it's all wrong.'

'Leave it, June. The less said the better.'

He could tell she was staring at him; but he was not going to turn his head.

'You've been squared up, haven't you?' she accused him. 'Well, it's not just down to you, Gordon. I'm the one who's had to put up with the gossip and the snide remarks, and I'm the one who's been grassed on by my guv'nor. I've got to have my own say in this.'

Her voice could be quite ugly when she was in a temper. This was something he had not encountered before. It wasn't the way he had wanted it all to finish. Finish, yes – it had been on the way out some weeks ago, if only their persecutors could have known – but not like this.

'The Monroe business,' he said. She really had to get this straight. 'Apparently he had nothing whatever to do with it.'

'Like hell.'

He was tempted to tell her the lot, in spite of what Derek Conway had said. But, snatching a glance at her, he knew that Conway had been all too accurate. There would be hell let loose on the DAC's doorstep, far worse than any demo in Trafalgar Square.

'You can think what you like, June,' he said as remotely as possible. 'But the fact is I'm biting the bullet on this one and keeping stum, and I'd like you to do the same.'

She said: 'Stop the car.'

'June . . .'

She was already undoing her safety belt. 'Stop this bloody car.'

188

He pulled up sharply. Somebody behind him let out an indignant hoot and swerved out in a tight arc. A face glared across at him. When he turned back towards June, she was getting out on to the pavement. All he could do was watch as she walked away, her shoulders set in anger and despair.

She would get over it, of course. Just as he would. Just as Angela would, if he played it clever. And he had been pretty lucky at playing it clever so far.

Until they all found out.

He wondered if he would ever be able to sit down and dispassionately work out whether it had all been worth it. June Ackland was diminishing in the distance. There was no way now he would even want to summon up the energy to chase after her.

There had to be some way of wiping the slate clean and making a new impressive mark in the next job.

Invitation to afternoon coffee in Chief Superintendent Brownlow's office could be flattering or disturbing, according to one's own assessment of one's own part in recent events. This afternoon Derek Conway felt tolerably relaxed. Brownlow was wearing his smug expression rather than that harassed one which boded ill for everyone in Sun Hill, starting at chief inspector level and working virulently downwards.

'A messy business, Derek.' Brownlow was in a mood to congratulate himself. 'But I think we managed to contain the damage.'

Conway was in favour of this benevolent attitude, but with a few reservations. 'I wouldn't be a hundred per cent sure we've heard the last of it, in every particular.'

'Oh, these things tend to rumble on for a while, but eventually the troops settle down and see sense.'

Conway was not going to let him get away quite so easily. 'One unfortunate side effect I should mention: there's a feeling in some quarters that to get on in a senior position at Sun Hill, you have to be on the square.'

'You and I can deny that wholeheartedly.'

'Well, we would say that, wouldn't we?' A vision of Wray's derisive, challenging features swam briefly in front of Conway's eyes. 'I mean,' he said hastily, 'that's what might be said by a critical outsider.'

Brownlow's good humour seemed impermeable. He looked, if anything, more pleased with himself than before. 'Our new DCI should put an end to all that nonsense.'

'You mean you've already got someone in mind?'

'I mean someone has been put into my mind, and I'm inclined to go along with the idea.'

'He's not a Mason?'

'Not a man,' said Brownlow complacently. 'Kim Reid, from the Fraud Squad. She's a very able officer.'

Conway mulled this over. At least, he supposed, having a woman in the post would mean that they were unlikely to have to go through today's unpleasantness again. Unless they were really out of luck.

At Sun Hill, luck was as unpredictable a commodity as the volume and variety of crime every hour of every day of every week. You could only wait and see, waking up each morning to cope with whatever landed on your plate – or to duck if it was too wildly wide of the plate.

A Selected List of Fiction Available from Mandarin

While every effort is made to keep prices low, it is sometimes necessary to increase prices at short notice. Mandarin Paperbacks reserves the right to show new retail prices on covers which may differ from those previously advertised in the text or elsewhere.

The prices shown below were correct at the time of going to press.

☐	7493 0003 5	**Mirage**	James Follett	£3.99
☐	7493 0134 1	**To Kill a Mockingbird**	Harper Lee	£2.99
☐	7493 0076 0	**The Crystal Contract**	Julian Rathbone	£3.99
☐	7493 0145 7	**Talking Oscars**	Simon Williams	£3.50
☐	7493 0118 X	**The Wire**	Nik Gowing	£3.99
☐	7493 0121 X	**Under Cover of Daylight**	James Hall	£3.50
☐	7493 0020 5	**Pratt of the Argus**	David Nobbs	£3.99
☐	7493 0097 3	**Second from Last in the Sack Race**	David Nobbs	£3.50

All these books are available at your bookshop or newsagent, or can be ordered direct from the publisher. Just tick the titles you want and fill in the form below.

Mandarin Paperbacks, Cash Sales Department, PO Box 11, Falmouth, Cornwall TR10 9EN.

Please send cheque or postal order, no currency, for purchase price quoted and allow the following for postage and packing:

UK   80p for the first book, 20p for each additional book ordered to a maximum charge of £2.00.

BFPO   80p for the first book, 20p for each additional book.

Overseas   £1.50 for the first book, £1.00 for the second and 30p for each additional book
including Eire thereafter.

NAME (Block letters) ....

ADDRESS ....

....

....